STONE ARCH BOOKS
a capstone imprint

BATMAN™
LI'L GOTHAM

STONE ARCH BOOKS™

Published in 2015 by Stone Arch Books
A Capstone Imprint
1710 Roe Crest Drive
North Mankato, MN 56003
www.capstonepub.com

Originally published by DC Comics in the U.S. in single magazine form as Batman: Li'l Gotham #12.

DC Comics
1700 Broadway, New York, NY 10019
A Warner Bros. Entertainment Company

Cataloging-in-Publication Data is available at the Library of Congress website:
ISBN: 978-1-4342-9737-2 (library binding)

Printed in China by Nordica.
0914/CA21401510
092014 008470NORDS15

Summary: Damian's fowlest friend Jerry has disappeared, but the people of Gotham City are not helping in his search for a missing turkey. Meanwhile, the Condiment King is making a Sandwich Day run! Then we close out the year with a bang before taking a long winter's nap, and Alfred goes through the family photo album with Damian.

STONE ARCH BOOKS
Ashley C. Andersen Zantop **Publisher**
Michael Dahl **Editorial Director**
Sean Tulien **Editor**
Heather Kindseth **Creative Director**
Bob Lentz **Art Director**
Hilary Wacholz and Peggie Carley **Designers**
Tori Abraham **Production Specialist**

DC Comics
Kristy Quinn **Original U.S. Editor**

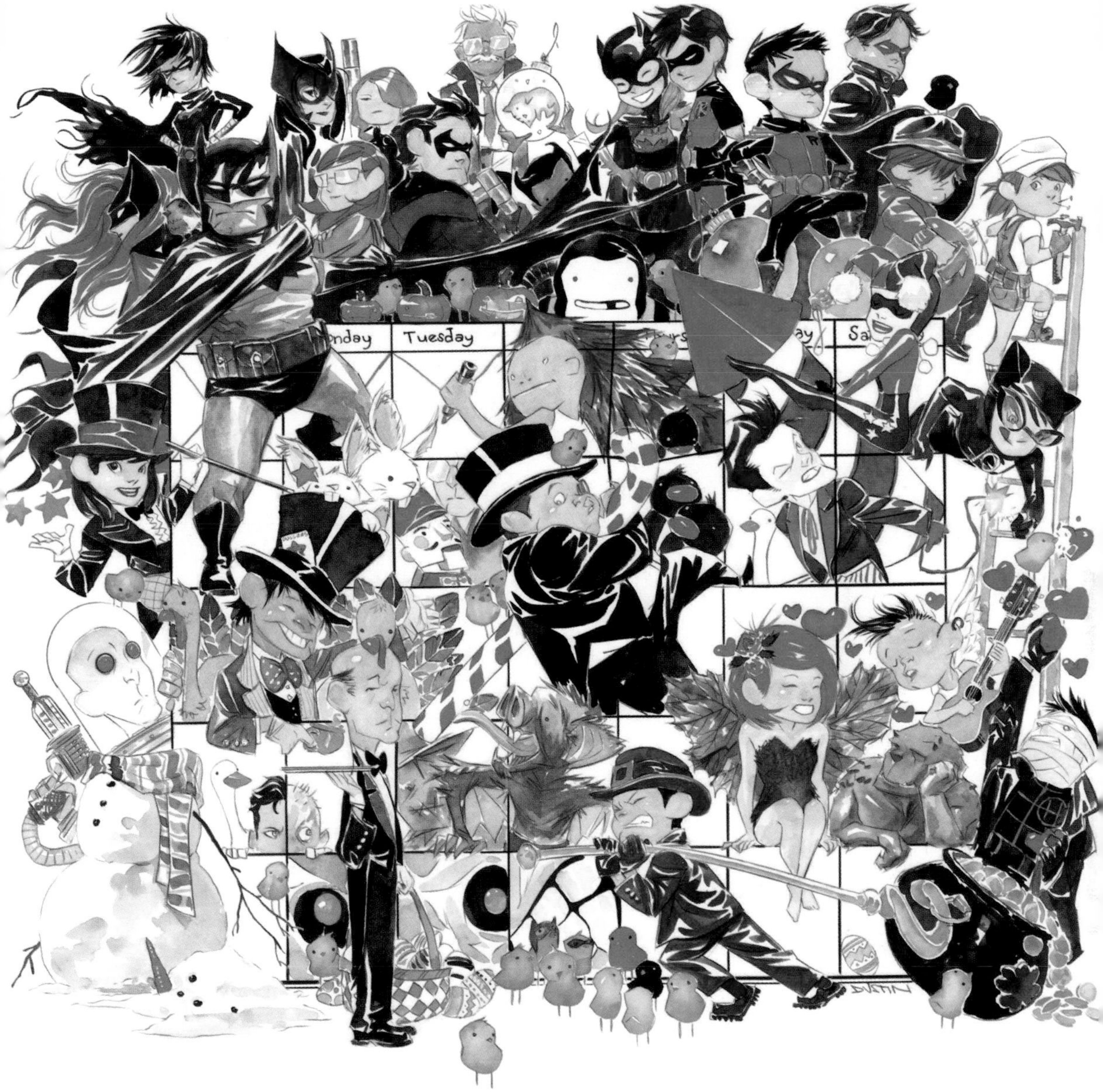
Tuesday
DUSTIN

SANDWICH DAY AND OUR FAMILY ALBUM

Dustin Nguyen & Derek Fridolfs...................... writers
Dustin Nguyen.. artist
Saida Temofonte.. letterer

BATMAN created by
Bob Kane

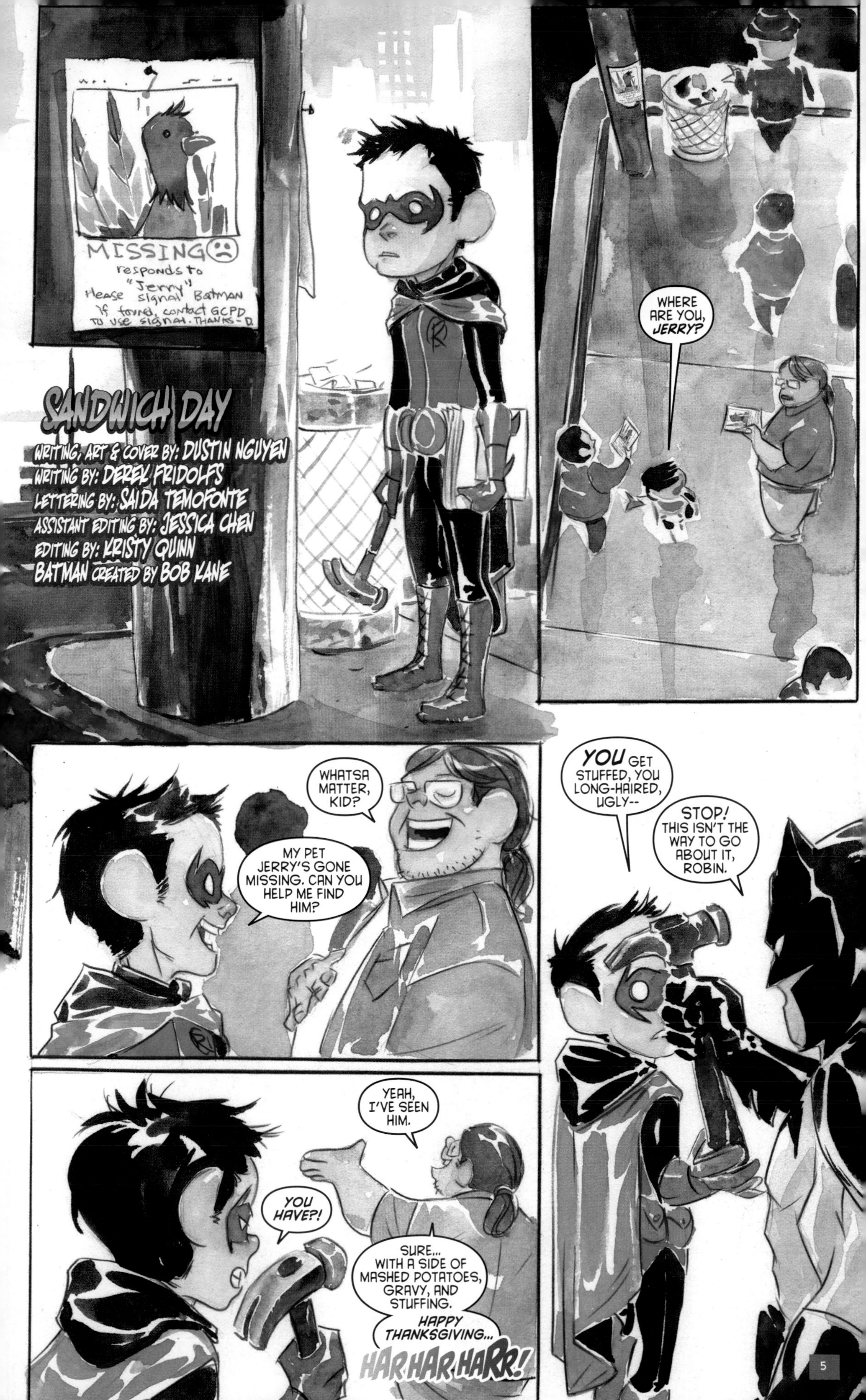
MISSING
responds to
"Jerry"
Please signal Batman
If found, contact GCPD
to use signal. Thanks - D.
SANDWICH DAY
WRITING, ART & COVER BY: DUSTIN NGUYEN
WRITING BY: DEREK FRIDOLFS
LETTERING BY: SAIDA TEMOFONTE
ASSISTANT EDITING BY: JESSICA CHEN
EDITING BY: KRISTY QUINN
BATMAN CREATED BY BOB KANE
WHERE ARE YOU, JERRY?
WHATSA MATTER, KID?
MY PET JERRY'S GONE MISSING. CAN YOU HELP ME FIND HIM?
YEAH, I'VE SEEN HIM.
YOU HAVE?!
SURE... WITH A SIDE OF MASHED POTATOES, GRAVY, AND STUFFING.
HAPPY THANKSGIVING...
HAR HAR HARR!
YOU GET STUFFED, YOU LONG-HAIRED, UGLY--
STOP! THIS ISN'T THE WAY TO GO ABOUT IT, ROBIN.

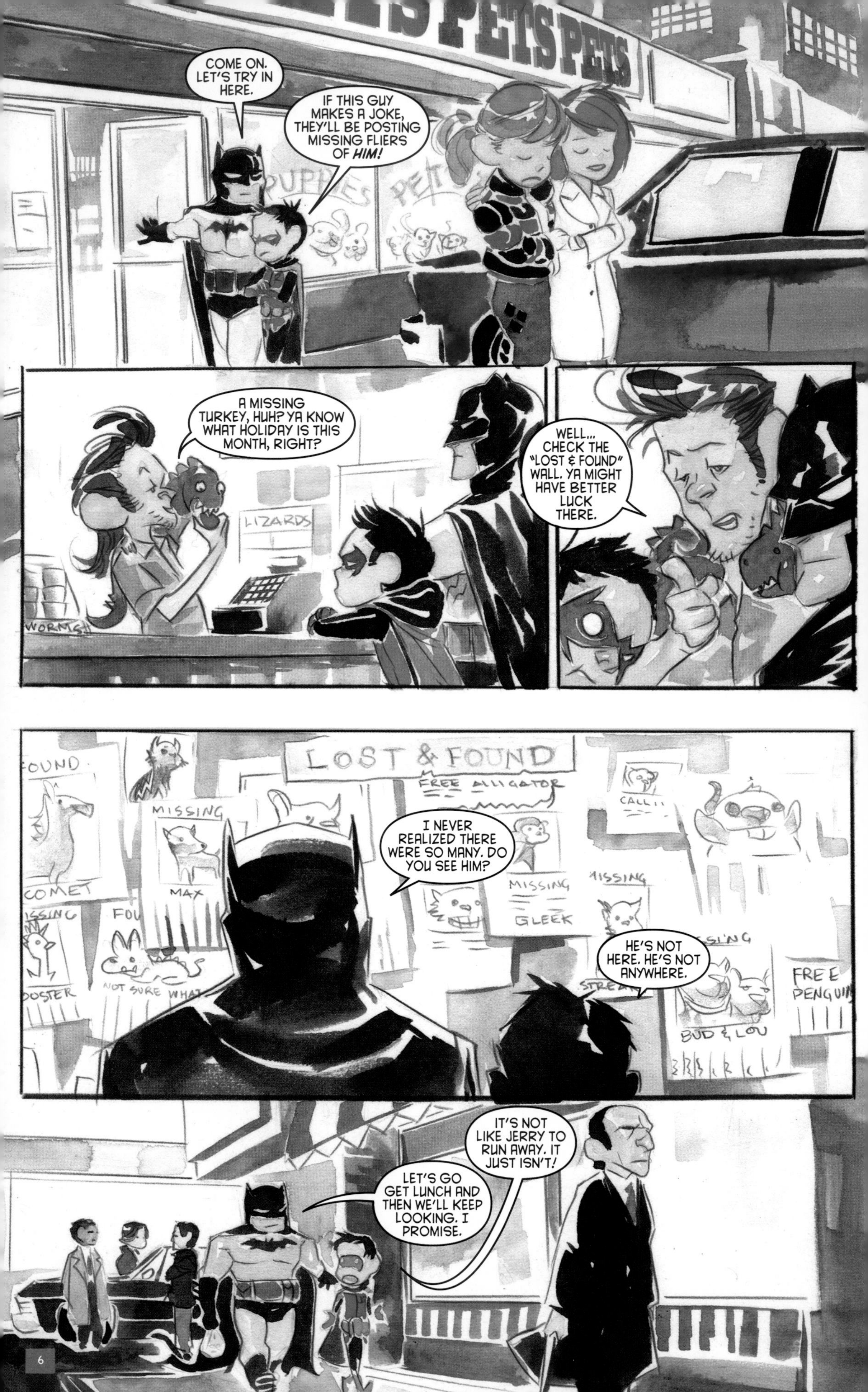

COME ON. LET'S TRY IN HERE.
IF THIS GUY MAKES A JOKE, THEY'LL BE POSTING MISSING FLIERS OF *HIM!*
A MISSING TURKEY, HUH? YA KNOW WHAT HOLIDAY IS THIS MONTH, RIGHT?
LIZARDS
WELL... CHECK THE "LOST & FOUND" WALL. YA MIGHT HAVE BETTER LUCK THERE.
LOST & FOUND
FREE ALLIGATOR
MISSING
COMET
MAX
I NEVER REALIZED THERE WERE SO MANY. DO YOU SEE HIM?
MISSING
GLEEK
NOT SURE WHAT
HE'S NOT HERE. HE'S NOT ANYWHERE.
BUD & LOU
IT'S NOT LIKE JERRY TO RUN AWAY. IT JUST ISN'T!
LET'S GO GET LUNCH AND THEN WE'LL KEEP LOOKING. I PROMISE.

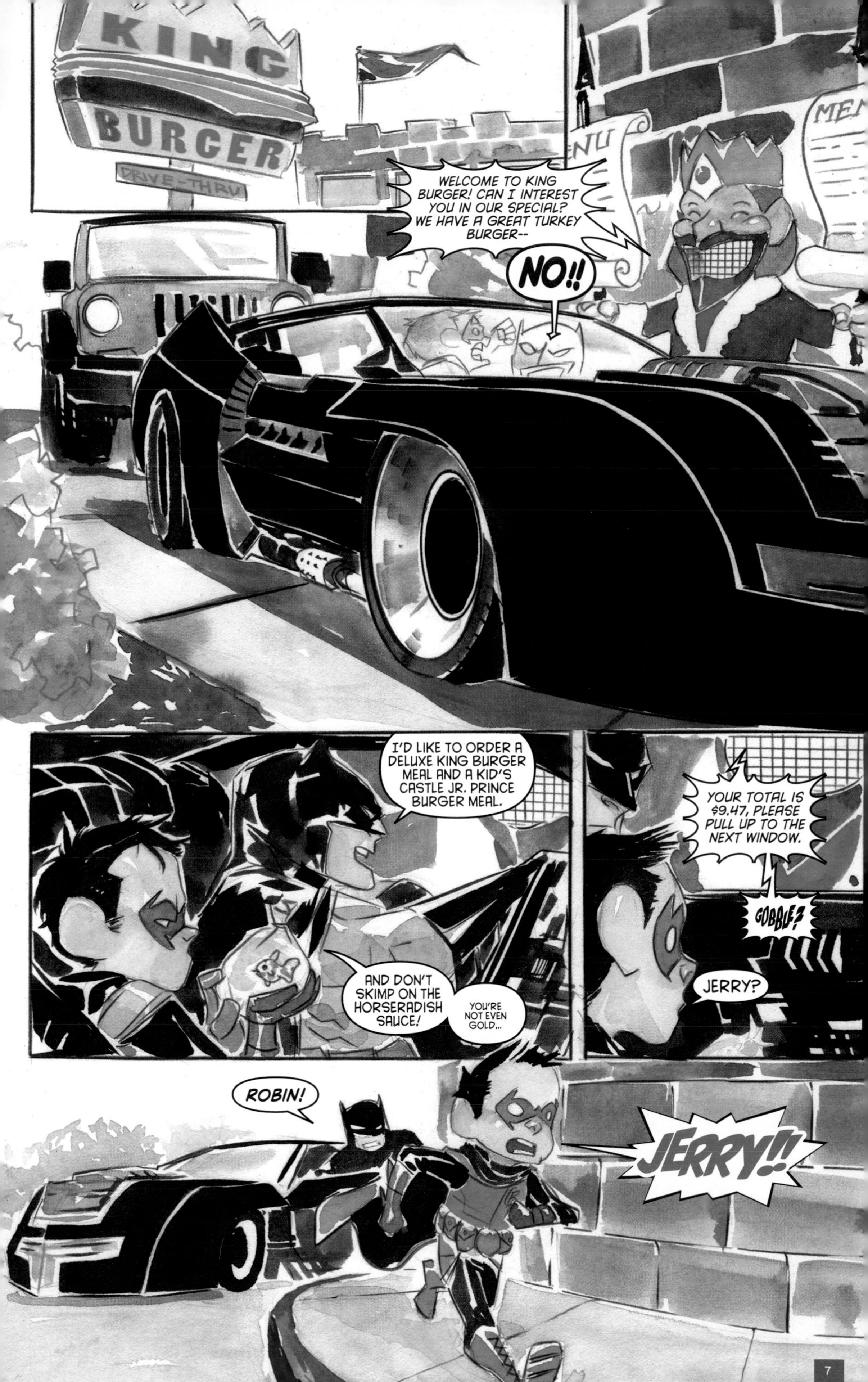
KING
BURGER
DRIVE-THRU
MENU
WELCOME TO KING BURGER! CAN I INTEREST YOU IN OUR SPECIAL? WE HAVE A GREAT TURKEY BURGER--
NO!!
I'D LIKE TO ORDER A DELUXE KING BURGER MEAL AND A KID'S CASTLE JR. PRINCE BURGER MEAL.
AND DON'T SKIMP ON THE HORSERADISH SAUCE!
YOU'RE NOT EVEN GOLD...
YOUR TOTAL IS $9.47, PLEASE PULL UP TO THE NEXT WINDOW.
GOBBLE?
JERRY?
ROBIN!
JERRY!!

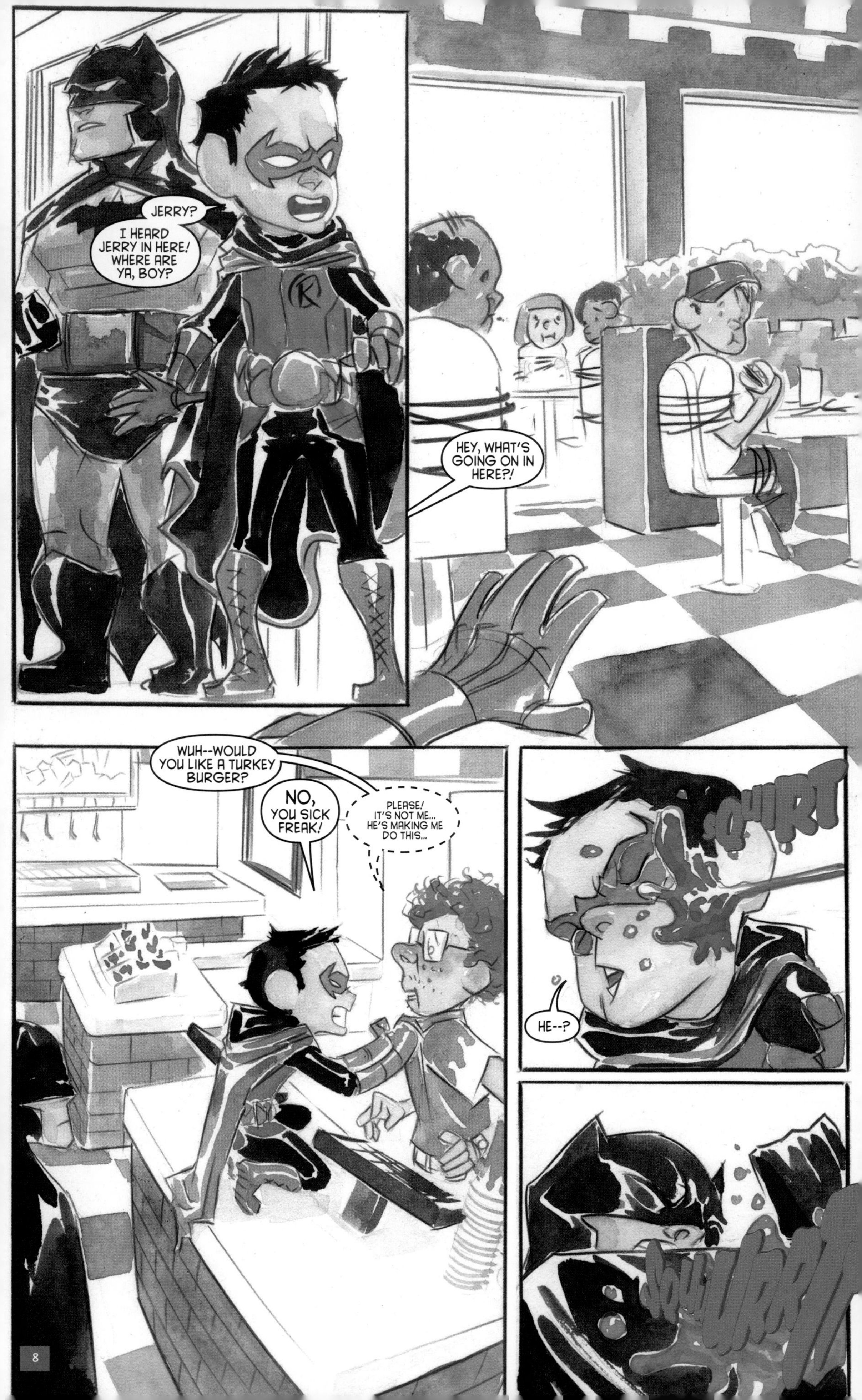
JERRY?
I HEARD JERRY IN HERE! WHERE ARE YA, BOY?
HEY, WHAT'S GOING ON IN HERE?!
WUH--WOULD YOU LIKE A TURKEY BURGER?
NO, YOU SICK FREAK!
PLEASE! IT'S NOT ME... HE'S MAKING ME DO THIS...
SQUIRT
HE--?
SQUUUIRT

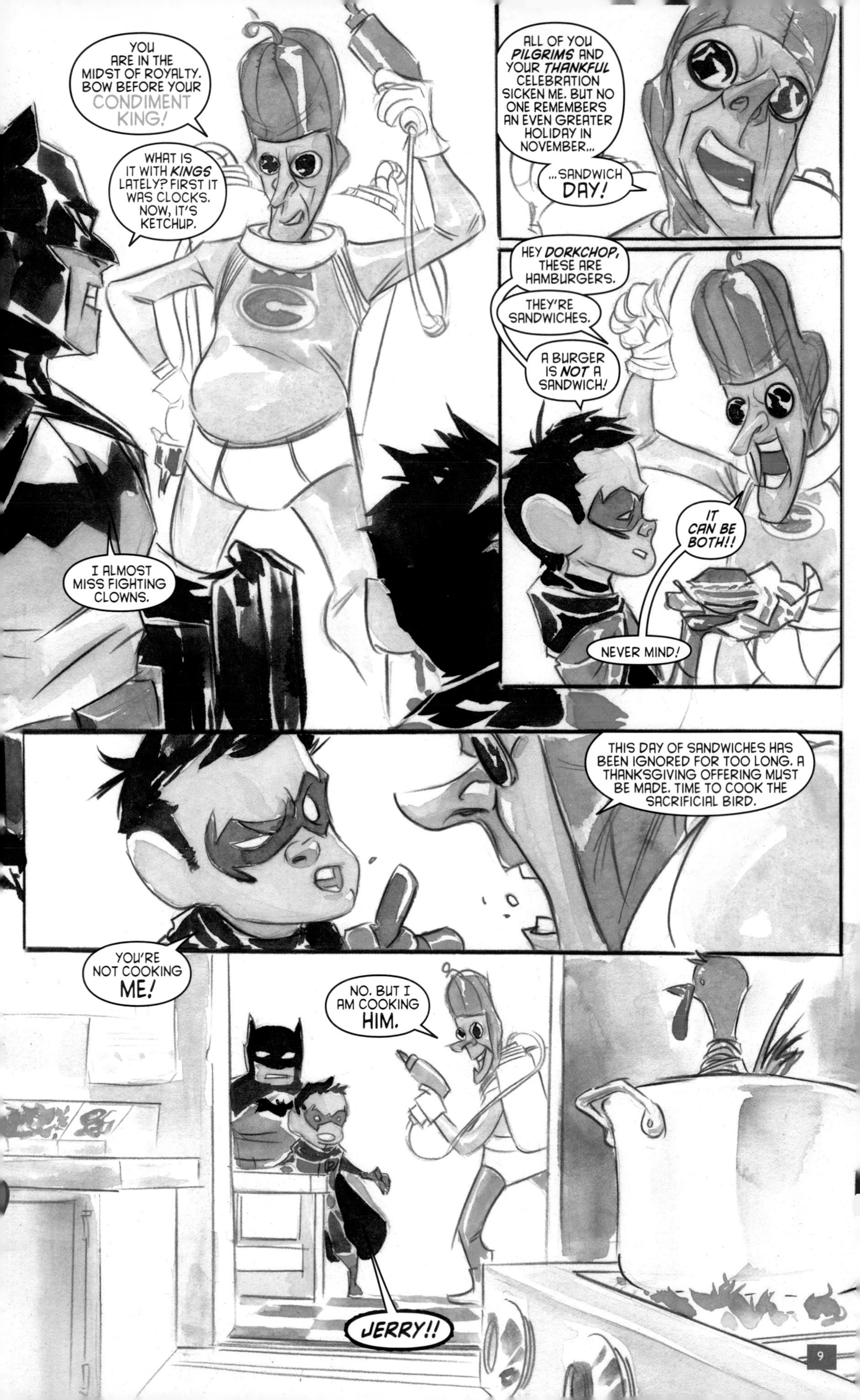
YOU ARE IN THE MIDST OF ROYALTY. BOW BEFORE YOUR CONDIMENT KING!
WHAT IS IT WITH KINGS LATELY? FIRST IT WAS CLOCKS. NOW, IT'S KETCHUP.
I ALMOST MISS FIGHTING CLOWNS.
ALL OF YOU PILGRIMS AND YOUR THANKFUL CELEBRATION SICKEN ME. BUT NO ONE REMEMBERS AN EVEN GREATER HOLIDAY IN NOVEMBER...
...SANDWICH DAY!
HEY DORKCHOP, THESE ARE HAMBURGERS.
THEY'RE SANDWICHES.
A BURGER IS NOT A SANDWICH!
IT CAN BE BOTH!!
NEVER MIND!
THIS DAY OF SANDWICHES HAS BEEN IGNORED FOR TOO LONG. A THANKSGIVING OFFERING MUST BE MADE. TIME TO COOK THE SACRIFICIAL BIRD.
YOU'RE NOT COOKING ME!
NO. BUT I AM COOKING HIM.
JERRY!!

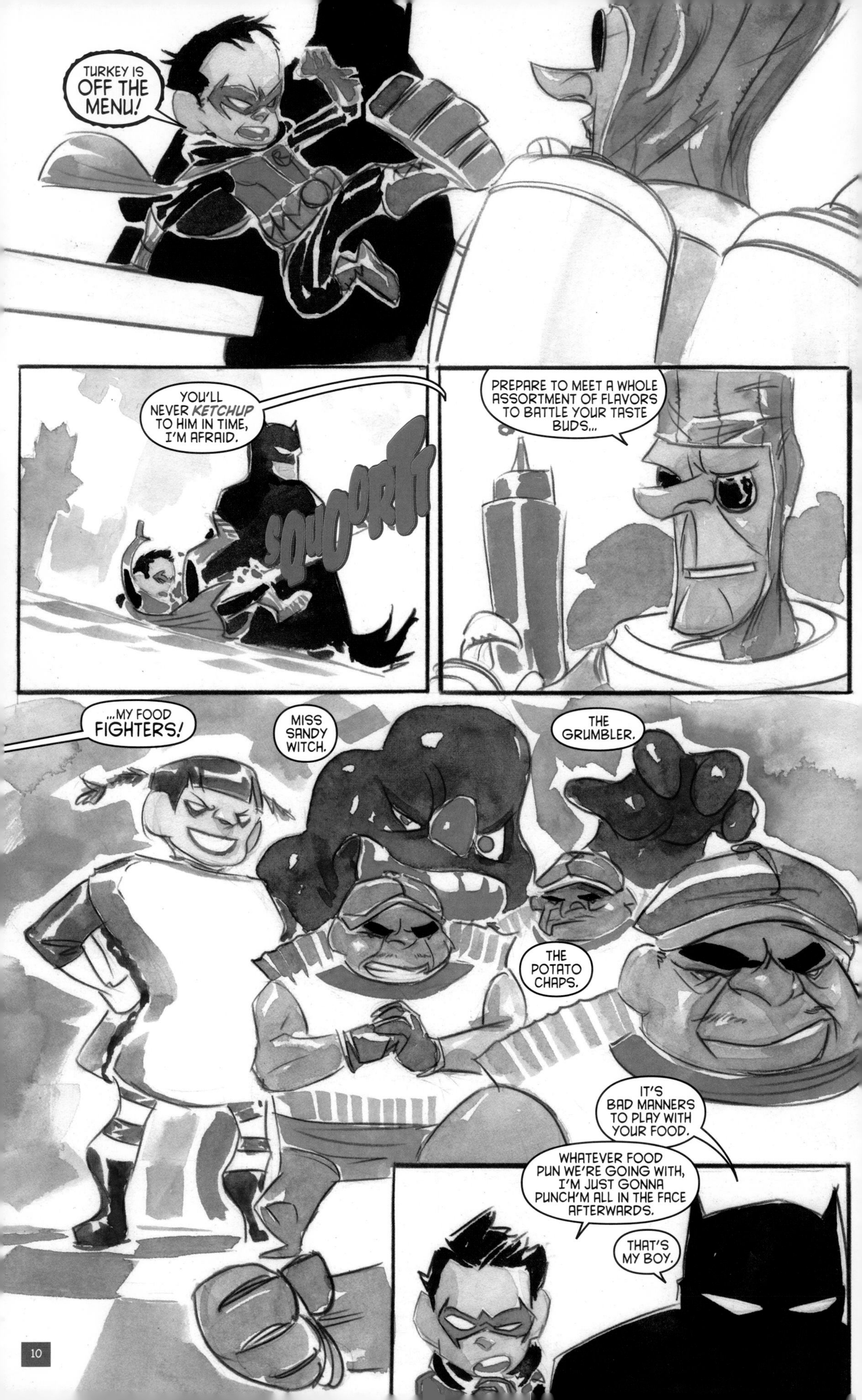
TURKEY IS OFF THE MENU!
YOU'LL NEVER KETCHUP TO HIM IN TIME, I'M AFRAID.
SQUOORT
PREPARE TO MEET A WHOLE ASSORTMENT OF FLAVORS TO BATTLE YOUR TASTE BUDS...
...MY FOOD FIGHTERS!
MISS SANDY WITCH.
THE GRUMBLER.
THE POTATO CHAPS.
IT'S BAD MANNERS TO PLAY WITH YOUR FOOD.
WHATEVER FOOD PUN WE'RE GOING WITH, I'M JUST GONNA PUNCH'M ALL IN THE FACE AFTERWARDS.
THAT'S MY BOY.

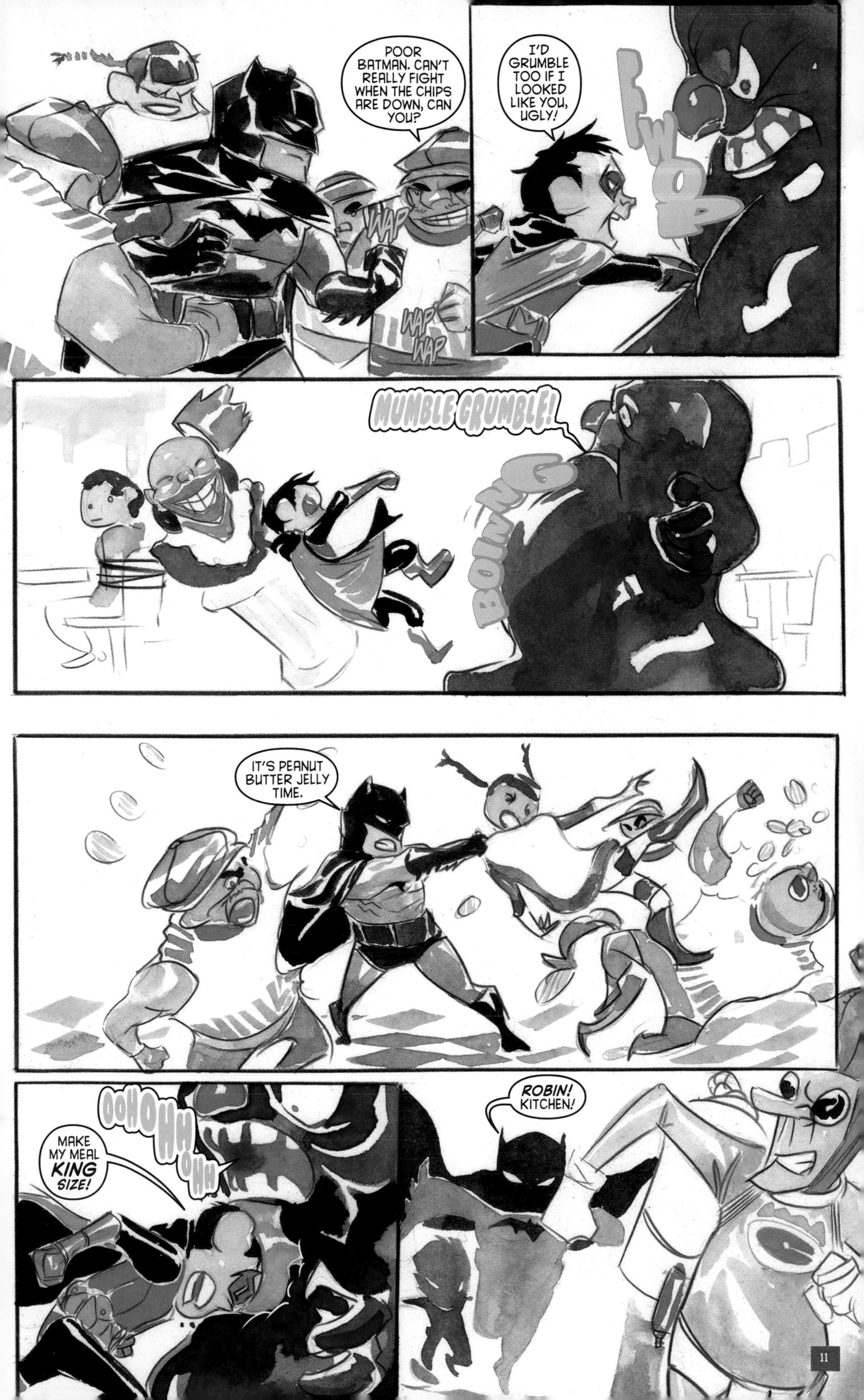
POOR BATMAN. CAN'T REALLY FIGHT WHEN THE CHIPS ARE DOWN, CAN YOU?
WAP
WAP
WAP
WAP
I'D GRUMBLE TOO IF I LOOKED LIKE YOU, UGLY!
FWOP
MUMBLE GRUMBLE!
BOING
IT'S PEANUT BUTTER JELLY TIME.
MAKE MY MEAL KING SIZE!
OOHOHHHOHH
ROBIN! KITCHEN!

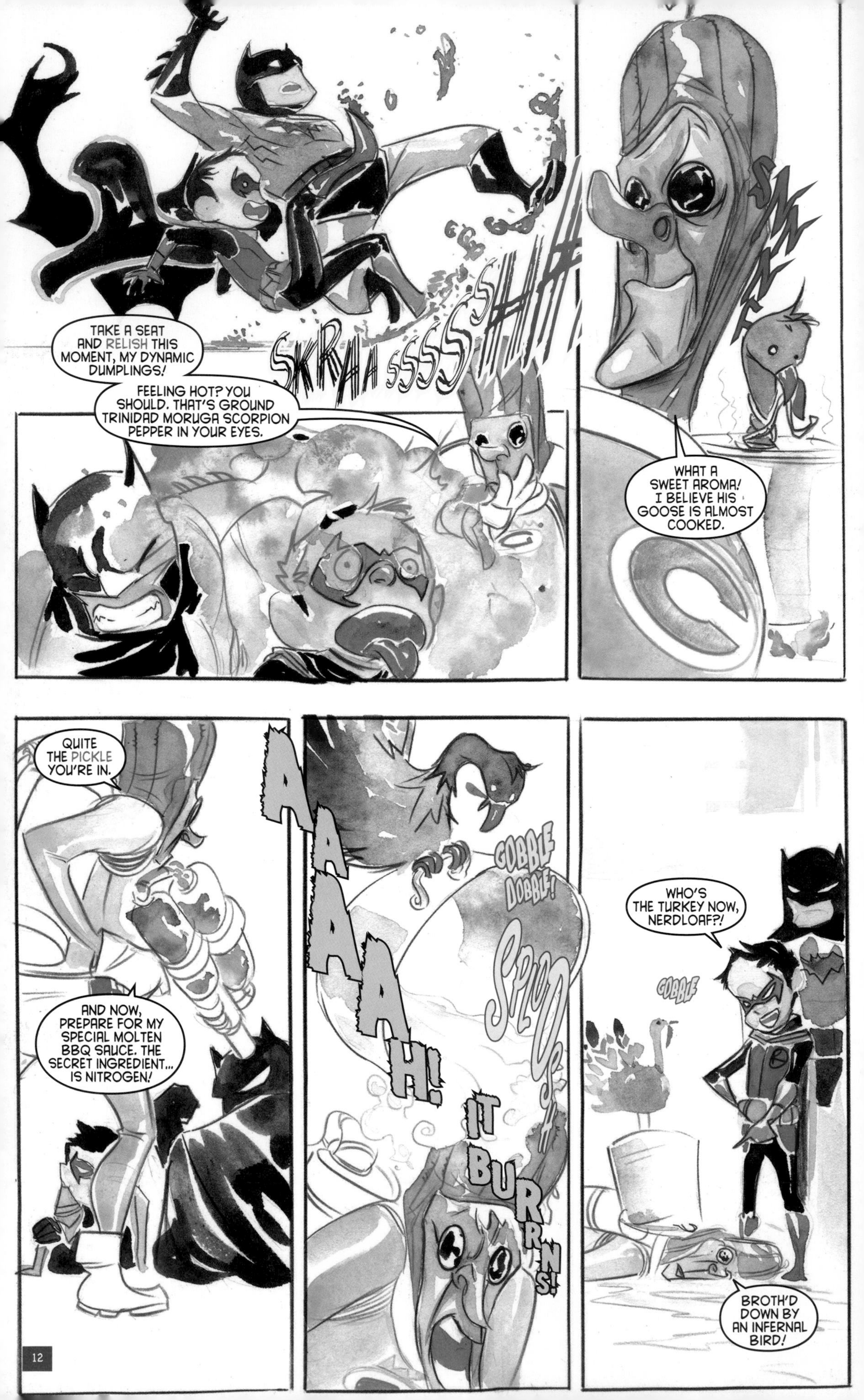
TAKE A SEAT AND RELISH THIS MOMENT, MY DYNAMIC DUMPLINGS!
SKRHA SSSSSSHHH
FEELING HOT? YOU SHOULD. THAT'S GROUND TRINIDAD MORUGA SCORPION PEPPER IN YOUR EYES.
WHAT A SWEET AROMA! I BELIEVE HIS GOOSE IS ALMOST COOKED.
QUITE THE PICKLE YOU'RE IN.
AND NOW, PREPARE FOR MY SPECIAL MOLTEN BBQ SAUCE. THE SECRET INGREDIENT... IS NITROGEN!
AAAAAAH!
GOBBLE DOBBLE!
IT BURRRNS!
WHO'S THE TURKEY NOW, NERDLOAF?!
GOBBLE
BROTH'D DOWN BY AN INFERNAL BIRD!

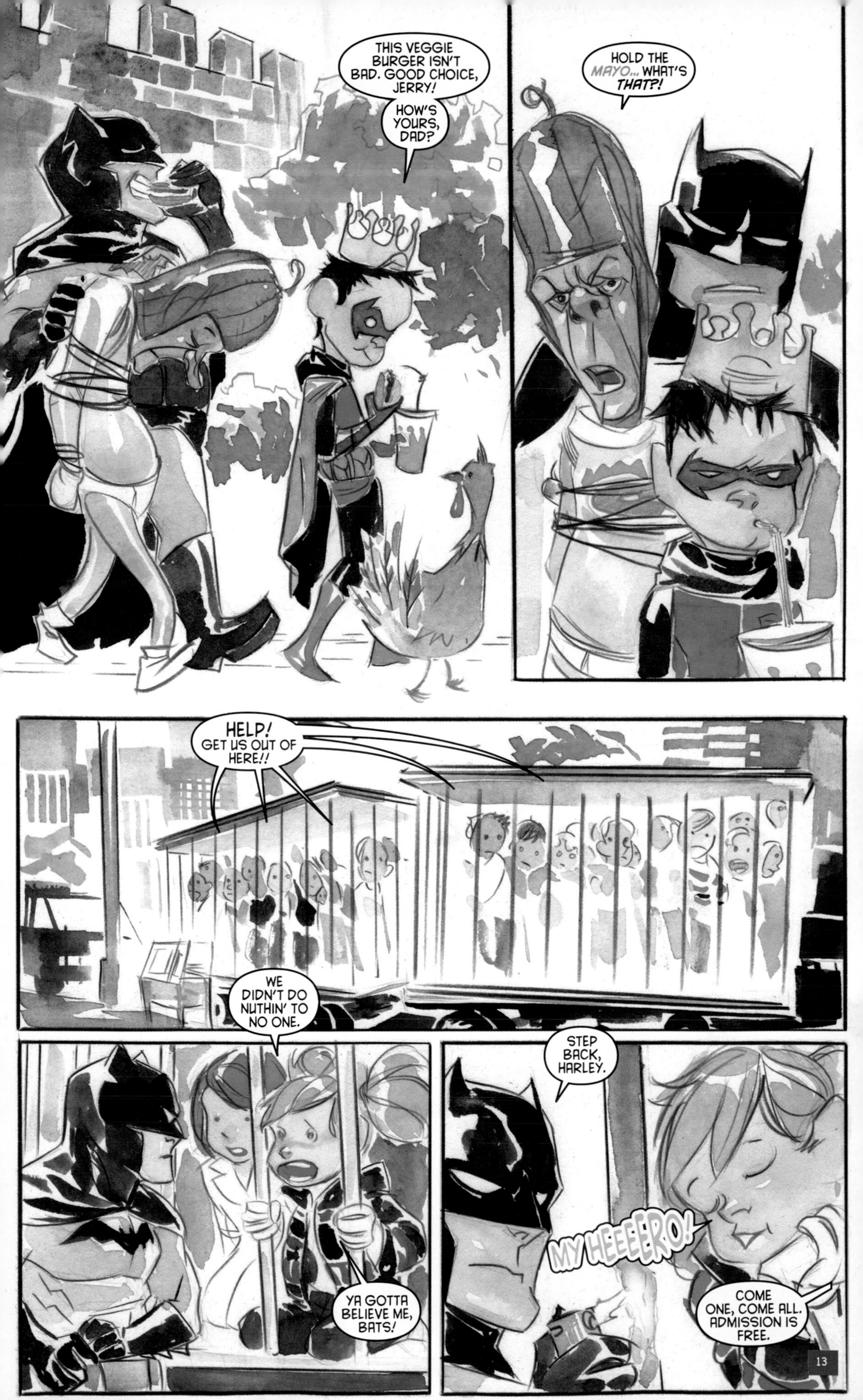
THIS VEGGIE BURGER ISN'T BAD. GOOD CHOICE, JERRY!
HOW'S YOURS, DAD?
HOLD THE MAYO... WHAT'S THAT?!
HELP! GET US OUT OF HERE!!
WE DIDN'T DO NUTHIN' TO NO ONE.
YA GOTTA BELIEVE ME, BATS!
STEP BACK, HARLEY.
MY HEEEERO!
COME ONE, COME ALL. ADMISSION IS FREE.

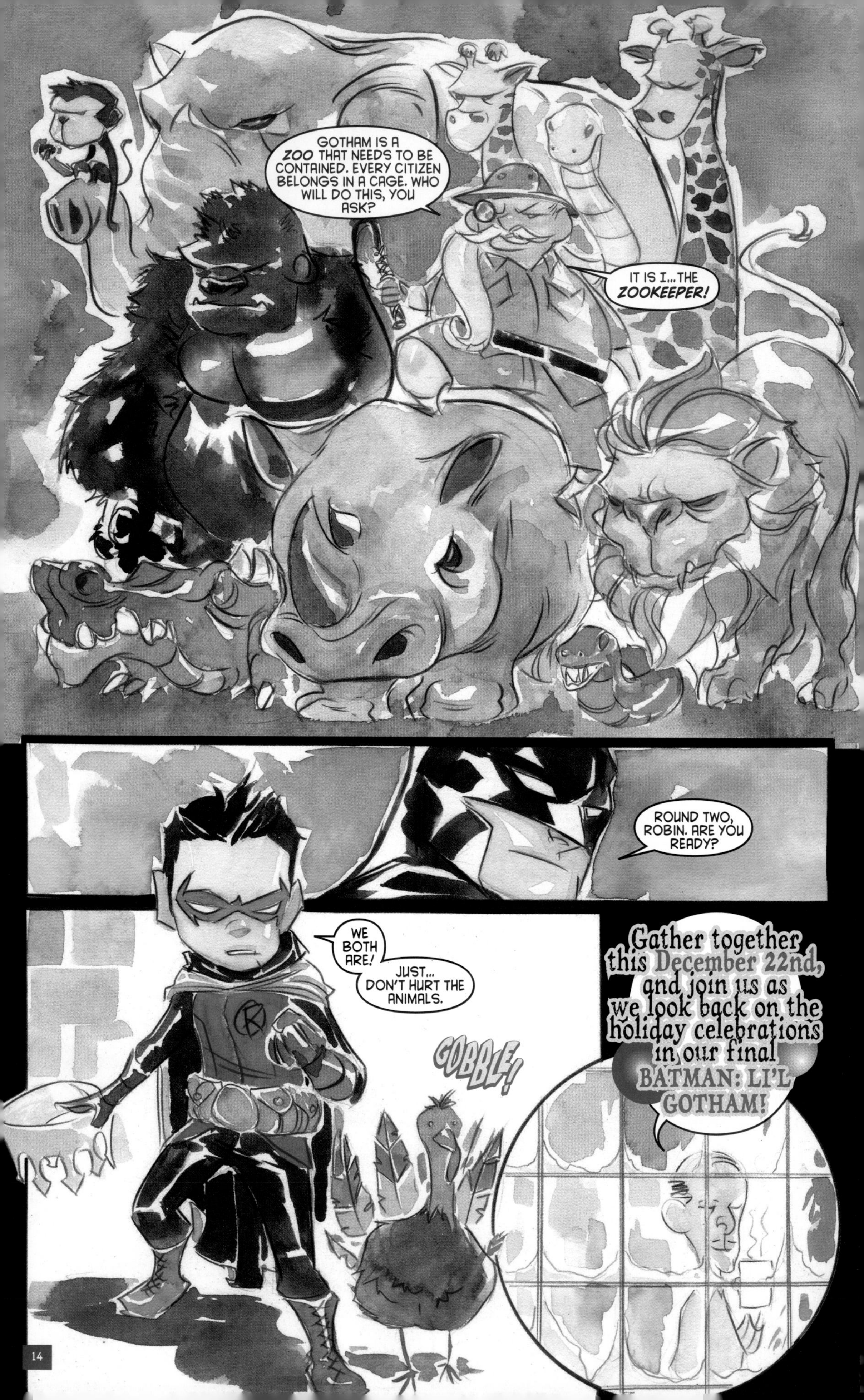
GOTHAM IS A ZOO THAT NEEDS TO BE CONTAINED. EVERY CITIZEN BELONGS IN A CAGE. WHO WILL DO THIS, YOU ASK?
IT IS I... THE ZOOKEEPER!
ROUND TWO, ROBIN. ARE YOU READY?
WE BOTH ARE!
JUST... DON'T HURT THE ANIMALS.
GOBBLE!
Gather together this December 22nd, and join us as we look back on the holiday celebrations in our final BATMAN: LI'L GOTHAM!

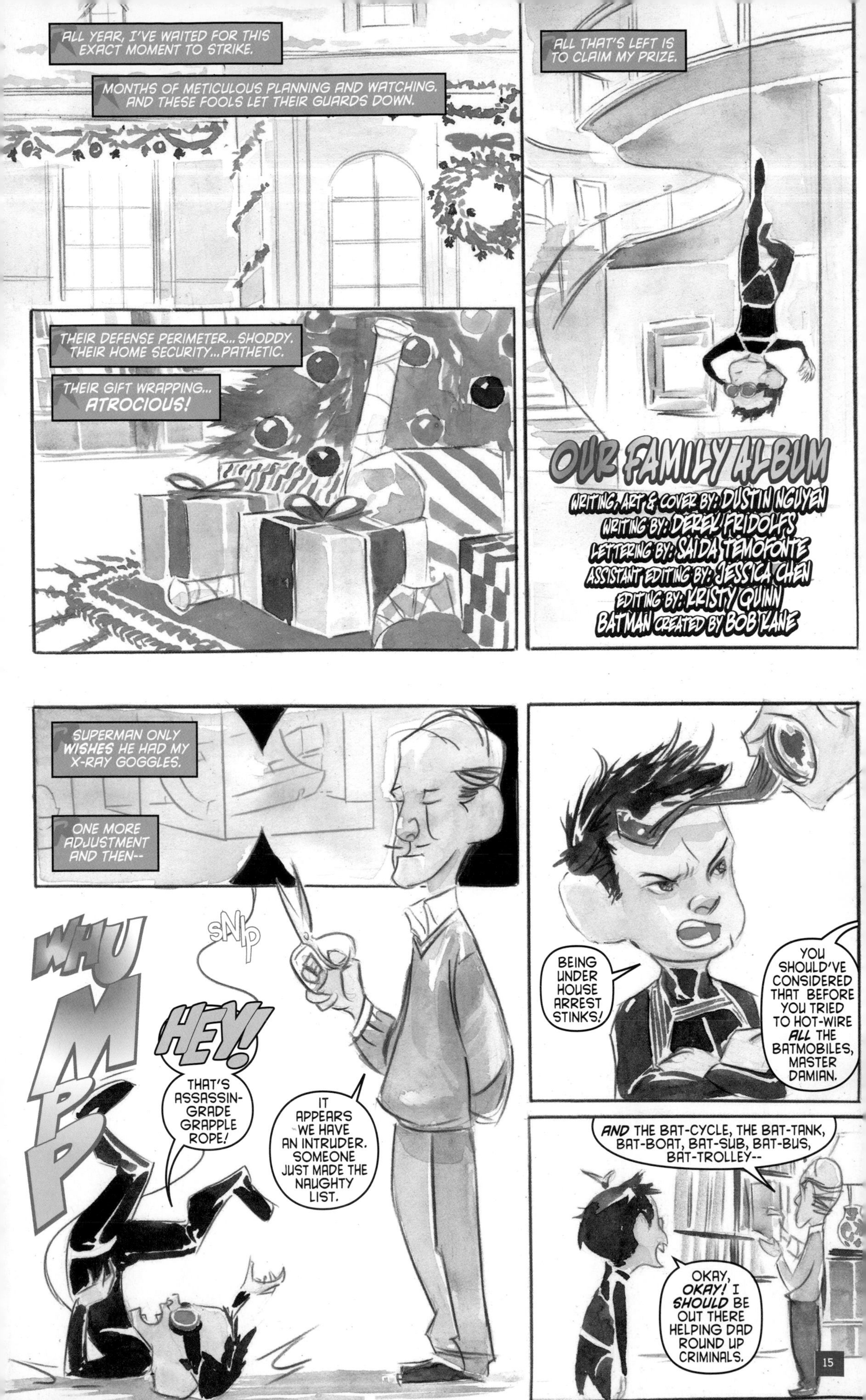

ALL YEAR, I'VE WAITED FOR THIS EXACT MOMENT TO STRIKE.
MONTHS OF METICULOUS PLANNING AND WATCHING. AND THESE FOOLS LET THEIR GUARDS DOWN.
ALL THAT'S LEFT IS TO CLAIM MY PRIZE.
THEIR DEFENSE PERIMETER... SHODDY. THEIR HOME SECURITY...PATHETIC.
THEIR GIFT WRAPPING... ATROCIOUS!
OUR FAMILY ALBUM
WRITING, ART & COVER BY: DUSTIN NGUYEN
WRITING BY: DEREK FRIDOLFS
LETTERING BY: SAIDA TEMOFONTE
ASSISTANT EDITING BY: JESSICA CHEN
EDITING BY: KRISTY QUINN
BATMAN CREATED BY BOB KANE
SUPERMAN ONLY WISHES HE HAD MY X-RAY GOGGLES.
ONE MORE ADJUSTMENT AND THEN--
SNIP
WHUMMPP
HEY!
THAT'S ASSASSIN-GRADE GRAPPLE ROPE!
IT APPEARS WE HAVE AN INTRUDER. SOMEONE JUST MADE THE NAUGHTY LIST.
BEING UNDER HOUSE ARREST STINKS!
YOU SHOULD'VE CONSIDERED THAT BEFORE YOU TRIED TO HOT-WIRE ALL THE BATMOBILES, MASTER DAMIAN.
AND THE BAT-CYCLE, THE BAT-TANK, BAT-BOAT, BAT-SUB, BAT-BUS, BAT-TROLLEY--
OKAY, OKAY! I SHOULD BE OUT THERE HELPING DAD ROUND UP CRIMINALS.

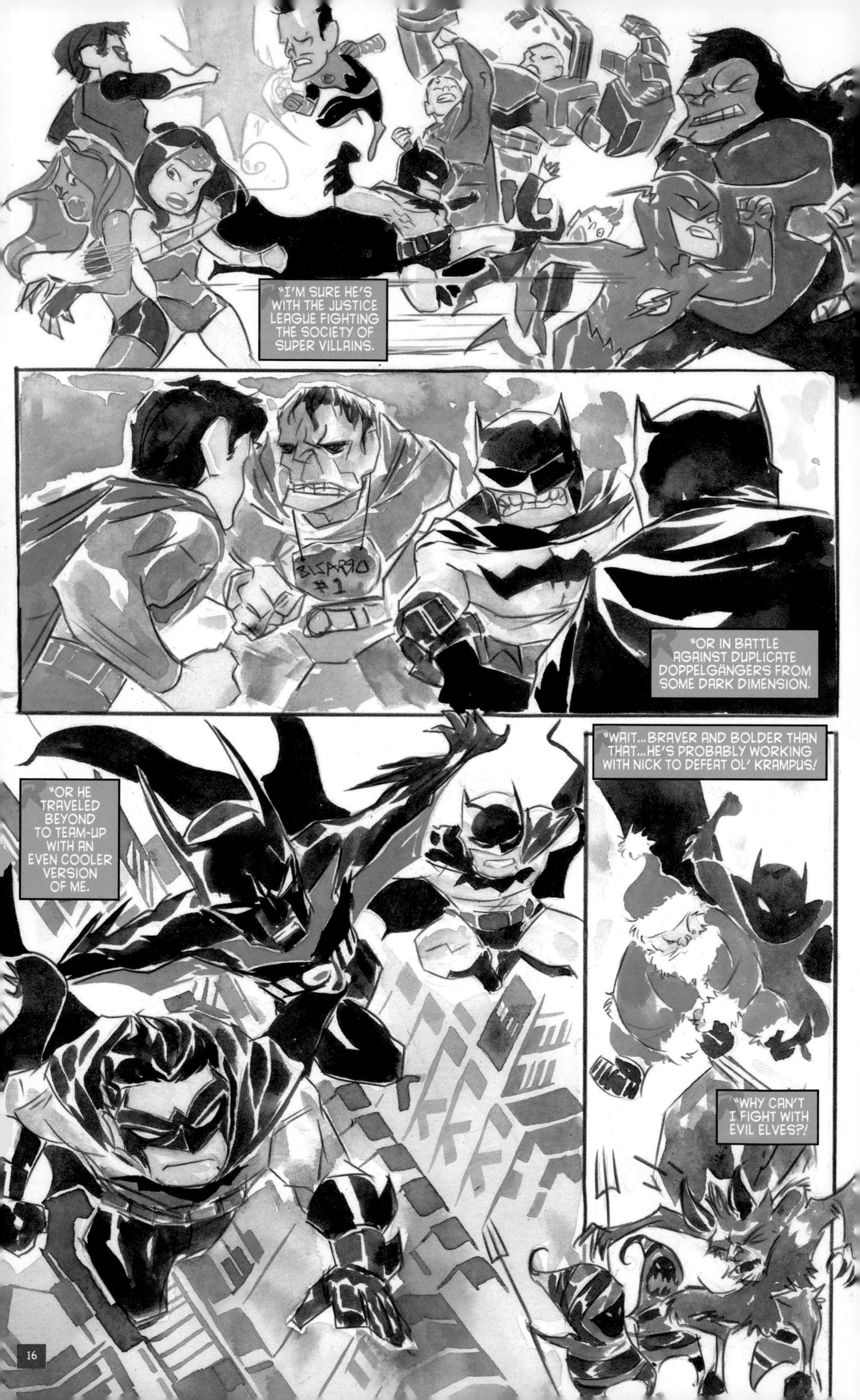
"I'M SURE HE'S WITH THE JUSTICE LEAGUE FIGHTING THE SOCIETY OF SUPER VILLAINS.
"OR IN BATTLE AGAINST DUPLICATE DOPPELGÄNGERS FROM SOME DARK DIMENSION.
"OR HE TRAVELED BEYOND TO TEAM-UP WITH AN EVEN COOLER VERSION OF ME.
"WAIT...BRAVER AND BOLDER THAN THAT...HE'S PROBABLY WORKING WITH NICK TO DEFEAT OL' KRAMPUS!
"WHY CAN'T I FIGHT WITH EVIL ELVES?!

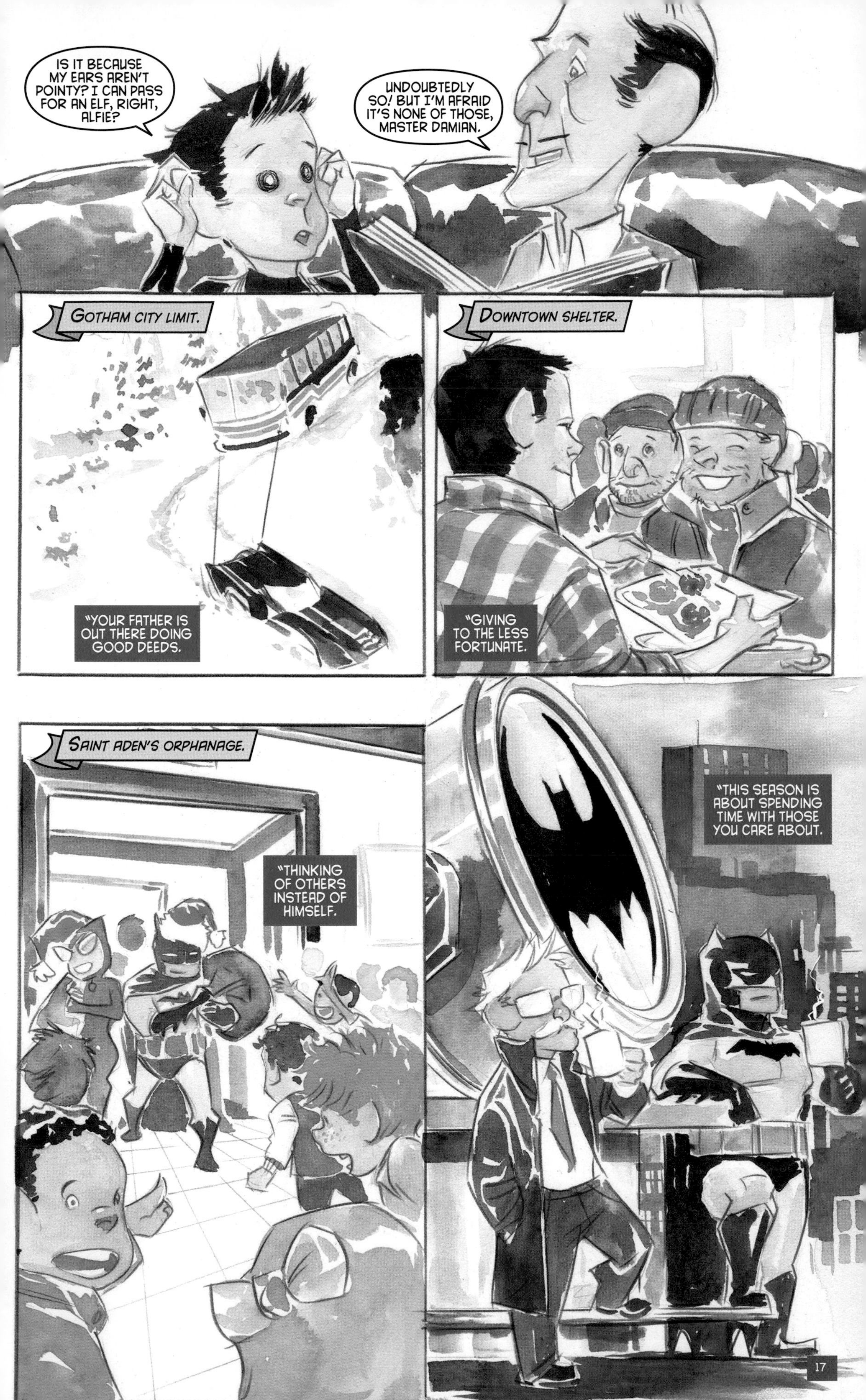
IS IT BECAUSE MY EARS AREN'T POINTY? I CAN PASS FOR AN ELF, RIGHT, ALFIE?
UNDOUBTEDLY SO! BUT I'M AFRAID IT'S NONE OF THOSE, MASTER DAMIAN.
GOTHAM CITY LIMIT.
"YOUR FATHER IS OUT THERE DOING GOOD DEEDS.
DOWNTOWN SHELTER.
"GIVING TO THE LESS FORTUNATE.
SAINT ADEN'S ORPHANAGE.
"THINKING OF OTHERS INSTEAD OF HIMSELF.
"THIS SEASON IS ABOUT SPENDING TIME WITH THOSE YOU CARE ABOUT.

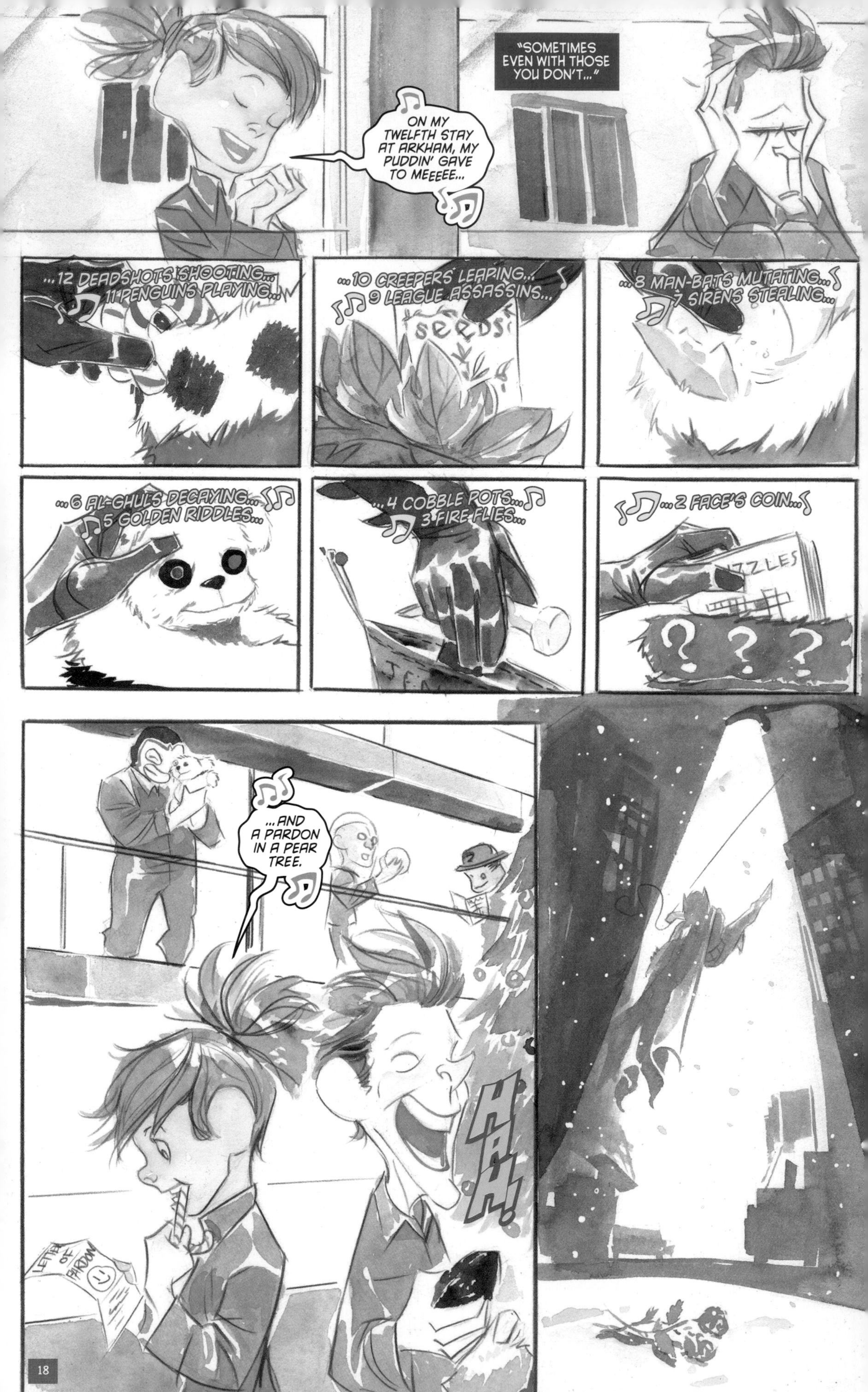

ON MY TWELFTH STAY AT ARKHAM, MY PUDDIN' GAVE TO MEEEEE...
"SOMETIMES EVEN WITH THOSE YOU DON'T..."
...12 DEADSHOTS SHOOTING... 11 PENGUINS PLAYING...
SEEDS
...10 CREEPERS LEAPING... 9 LEAGUE ASSASSINS...
...8 MAN-BATS MUTATING... 7 SIRENS STEALING...
...6 AL-GHULS DECAYING... 5 GOLDEN RIDDLES...
...4 COBBLE POTS... 3 FIRE FLIES...
...2 FACE'S COIN...
...AND A PARDON IN A PEAR TREE.
LETTER OF PARDON
HAH!

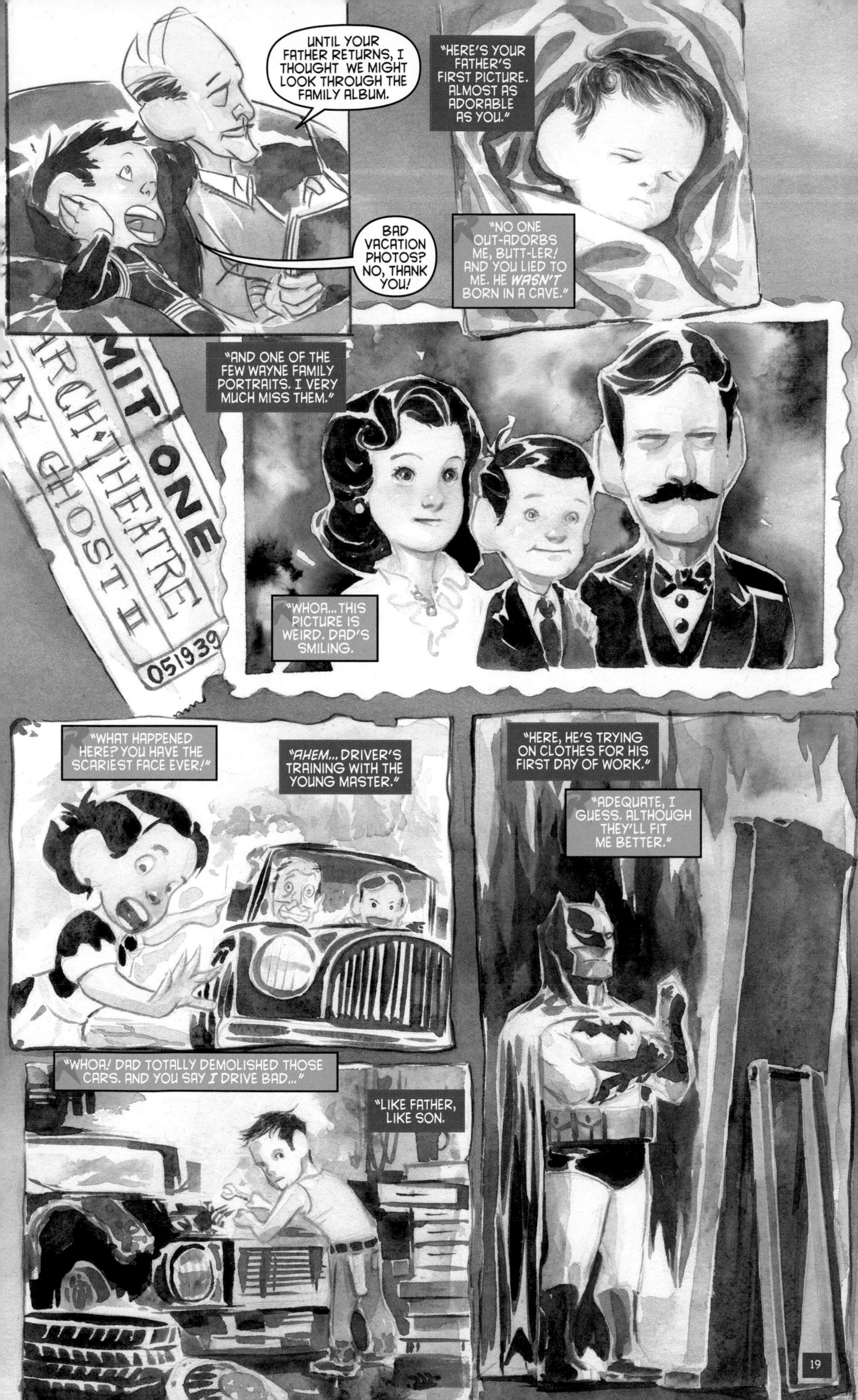
UNTIL YOUR FATHER RETURNS, I THOUGHT WE MIGHT LOOK THROUGH THE FAMILY ALBUM.
BAD VACATION PHOTOS? NO, THANK YOU!
"HERE'S YOUR FATHER'S FIRST PICTURE. ALMOST AS ADORABLE AS YOU."
"NO ONE OUT-ADORBS ME, BUTT-LER! AND YOU LIED TO ME. HE WASN'T BORN IN A CAVE."
"AND ONE OF THE FEW WAYNE FAMILY PORTRAITS. I VERY MUCH MISS THEM."
MIT ONE
ARCH THEATRE
AY GHOST II
051939
"WHOA... THIS PICTURE IS WEIRD. DAD'S SMILING.
"WHAT HAPPENED HERE? YOU HAVE THE SCARIEST FACE EVER!"
"AHEM... DRIVER'S TRAINING WITH THE YOUNG MASTER."
"WHOA! DAD TOTALLY DEMOLISHED THOSE CARS. AND YOU SAY I DRIVE BAD..."
"LIKE FATHER, LIKE SON.
"HERE, HE'S TRYING ON CLOTHES FOR HIS FIRST DAY OF WORK."
"ADEQUATE, I GUESS. ALTHOUGH THEY'LL FIT ME BETTER."

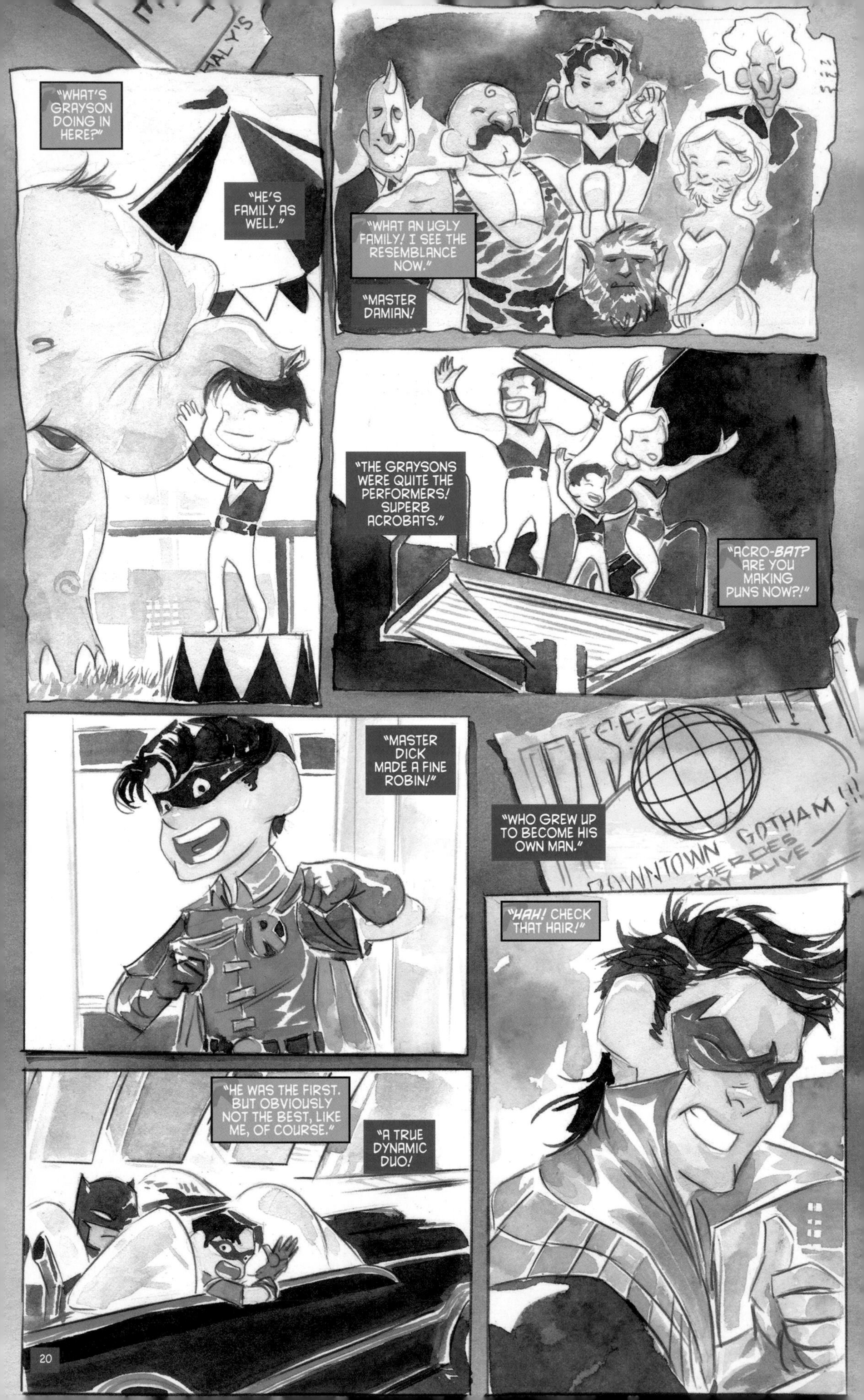
HALY'S
"WHAT'S GRAYSON DOING IN HERE?"
"HE'S FAMILY AS WELL."
"WHAT AN UGLY FAMILY! I SEE THE RESEMBLANCE NOW."
"MASTER DAMIAN!
"THE GRAYSONS WERE QUITE THE PERFORMERS! SUPERB ACROBATS."
"ACRO-*BAT?* ARE YOU MAKING PUNS NOW?!"
"MASTER DICK MADE A FINE ROBIN!"
"WHO GREW UP TO BECOME HIS OWN MAN."
"*HAH!* CHECK THAT HAIR!"
"HE WAS THE FIRST. BUT OBVIOUSLY NOT THE BEST, LIKE ME, OF COURSE."
"A TRUE DYNAMIC DUO!

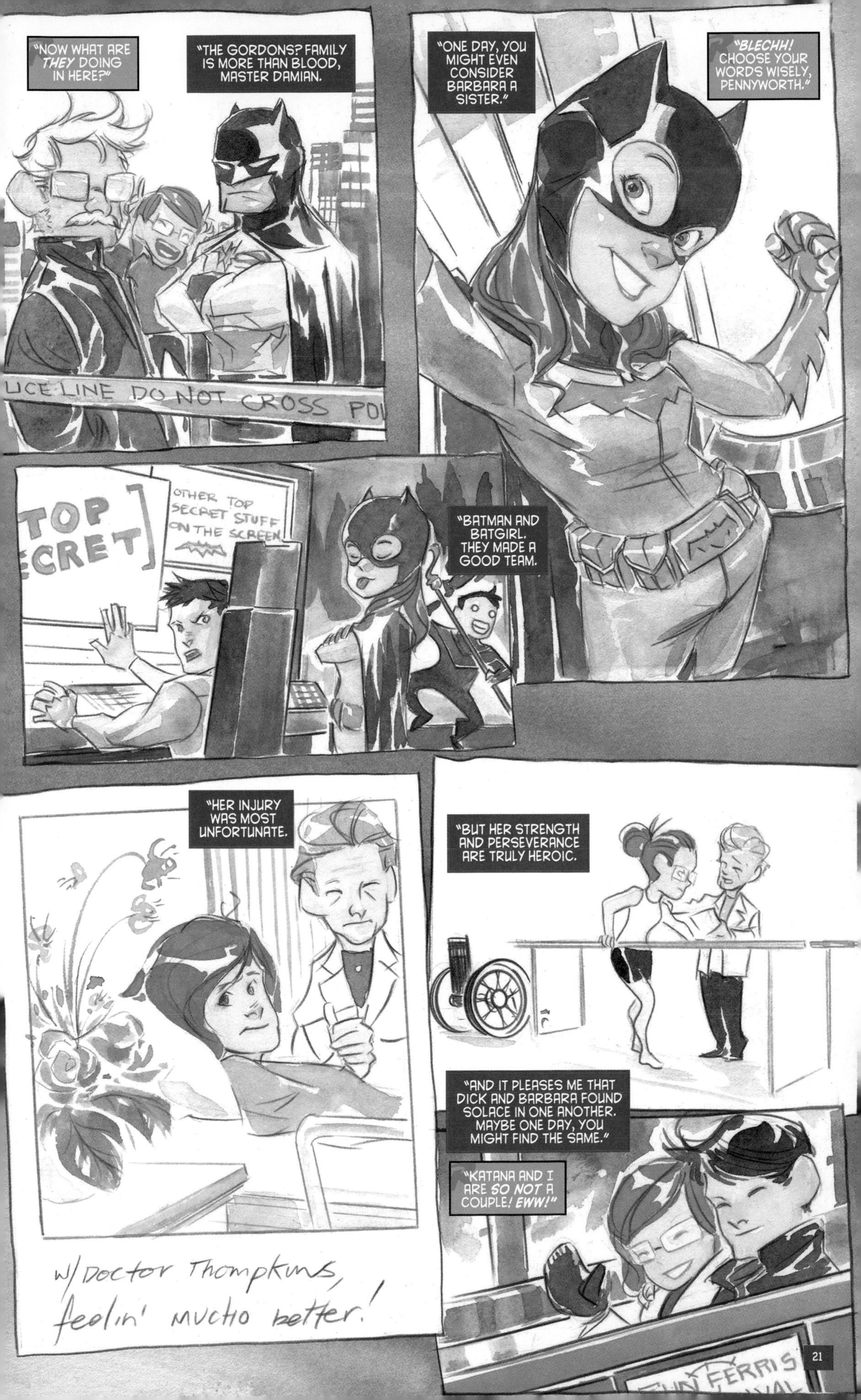
"NOW WHAT ARE *THEY* DOING IN HERE?"
"THE GORDONS? FAMILY IS MORE THAN BLOOD, MASTER DAMIAN.
UCE LINE DO NOT CROSS PO
"ONE DAY, YOU MIGHT EVEN CONSIDER BARBARA A SISTER."
"*BLECHH!* CHOOSE YOUR WORDS WISELY, PENNYWORTH."
TOP
CRET
OTHER TOP SECRET STUFF ON THE SCREEN
"BATMAN AND BATGIRL. THEY MADE A GOOD TEAM.
"HER INJURY WAS MOST UNFORTUNATE.
w/ Doctor Thompkins, feelin' mucho better!
"BUT HER STRENGTH AND PERSEVERANCE ARE TRULY HEROIC.
"AND IT PLEASES ME THAT DICK AND BARBARA FOUND SOLACE IN ONE ANOTHER. MAYBE ONE DAY, YOU MIGHT FIND THE SAME."
"KATANA AND I ARE *SO NOT* A COUPLE! *EWW!*"

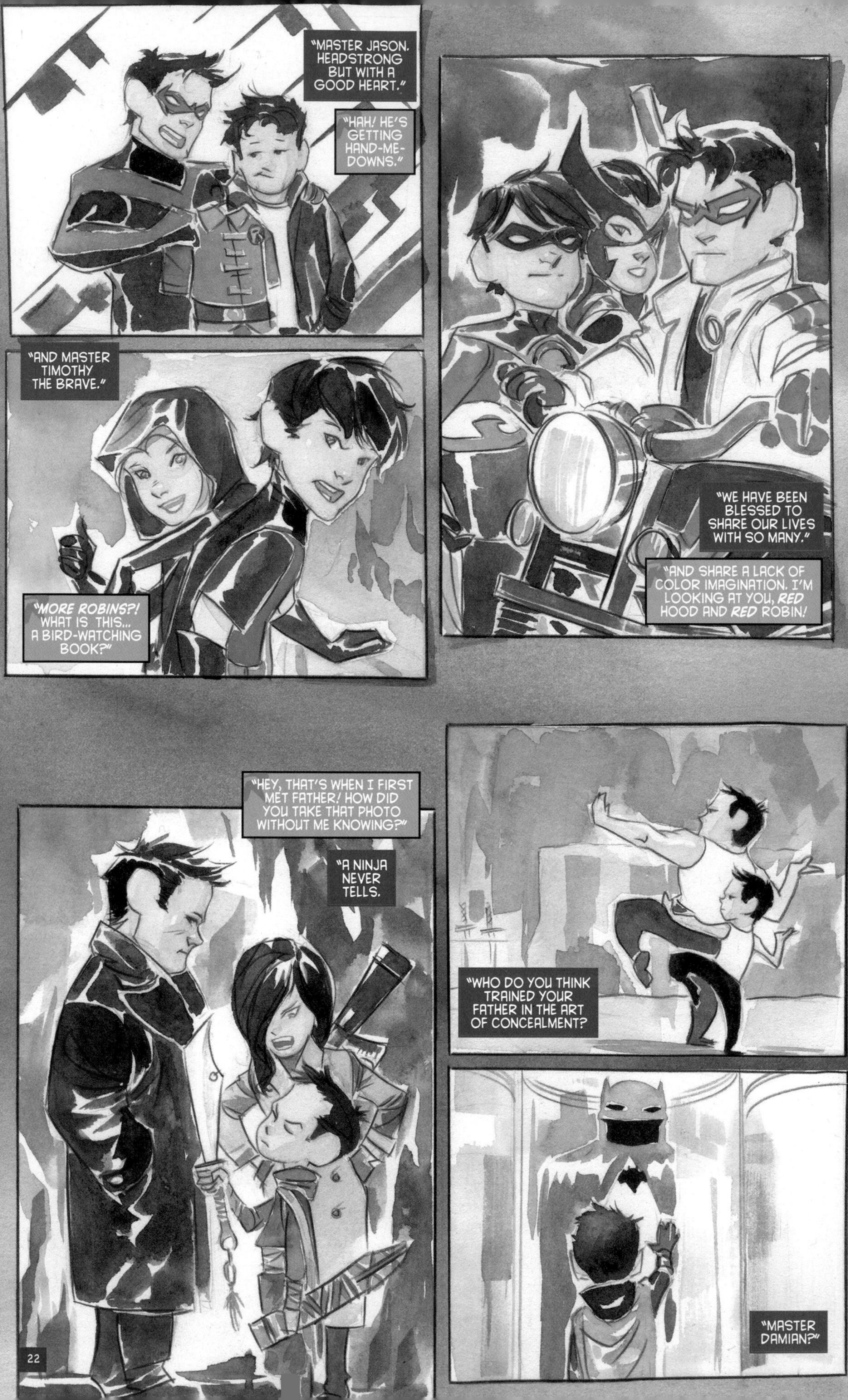
"MASTER JASON. HEADSTRONG BUT WITH A GOOD HEART."
"HAH! HE'S GETTING HAND-ME-DOWNS."
"AND MASTER TIMOTHY THE BRAVE."
"MORE ROBINS?! WHAT IS THIS... A BIRD-WATCHING BOOK?"
"WE HAVE BEEN BLESSED TO SHARE OUR LIVES WITH SO MANY."
"AND SHARE A LACK OF COLOR IMAGINATION. I'M LOOKING AT YOU, RED HOOD AND RED ROBIN!
"HEY, THAT'S WHEN I FIRST MET FATHER! HOW DID YOU TAKE THAT PHOTO WITHOUT ME KNOWING?"
"A NINJA NEVER TELLS.
"WHO DO YOU THINK TRAINED YOUR FATHER IN THE ART OF CONCEALMENT?
"MASTER DAMIAN?"

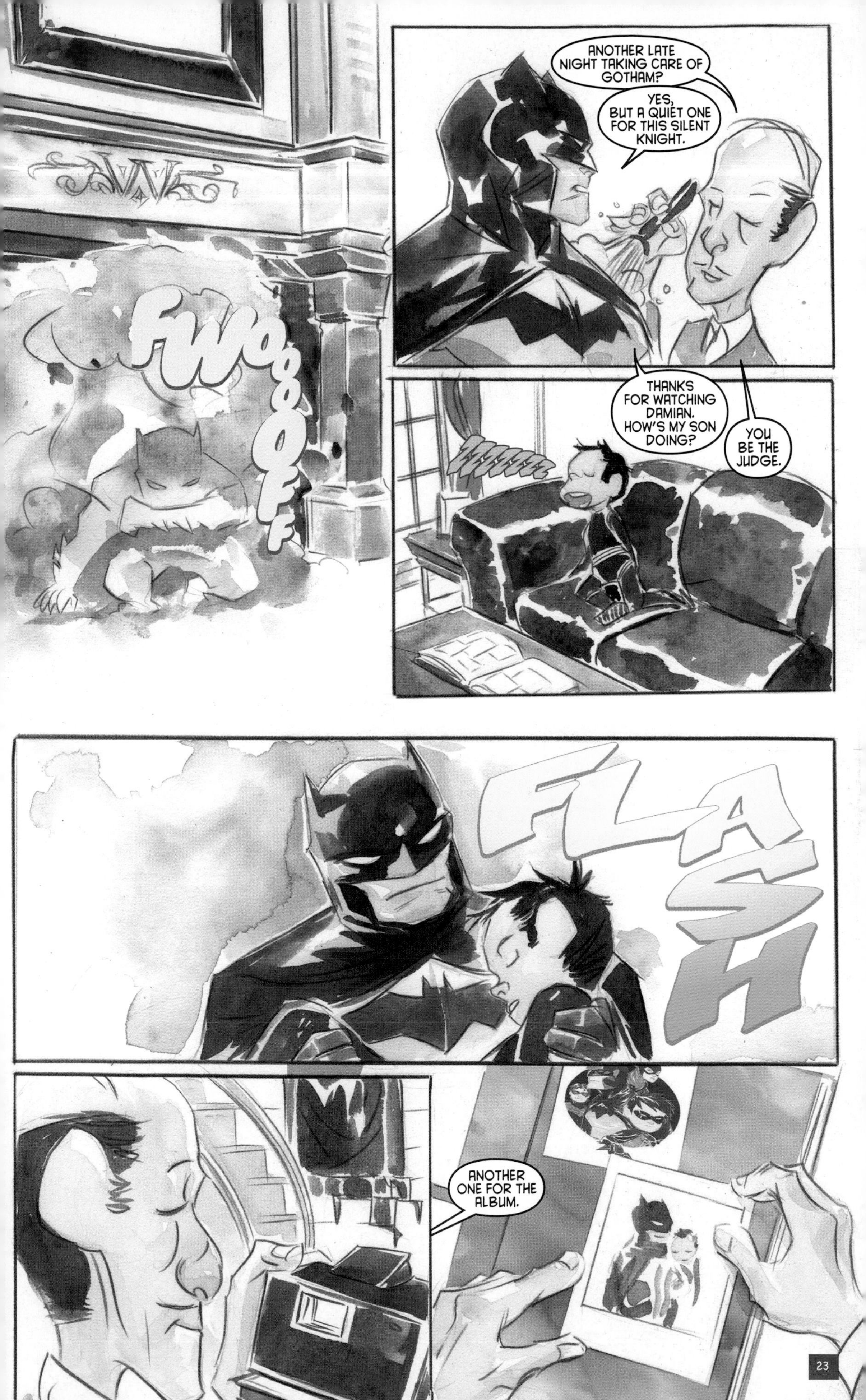
FWOOOOOFF
ANOTHER LATE NIGHT TAKING CARE OF GOTHAM?
YES, BUT A QUIET ONE FOR THIS SILENT KNIGHT.
THANKS FOR WATCHING DAMIAN. HOW'S MY SON DOING?
YOU BE THE JUDGE.
FLASH
ANOTHER ONE FOR THE ALBUM.

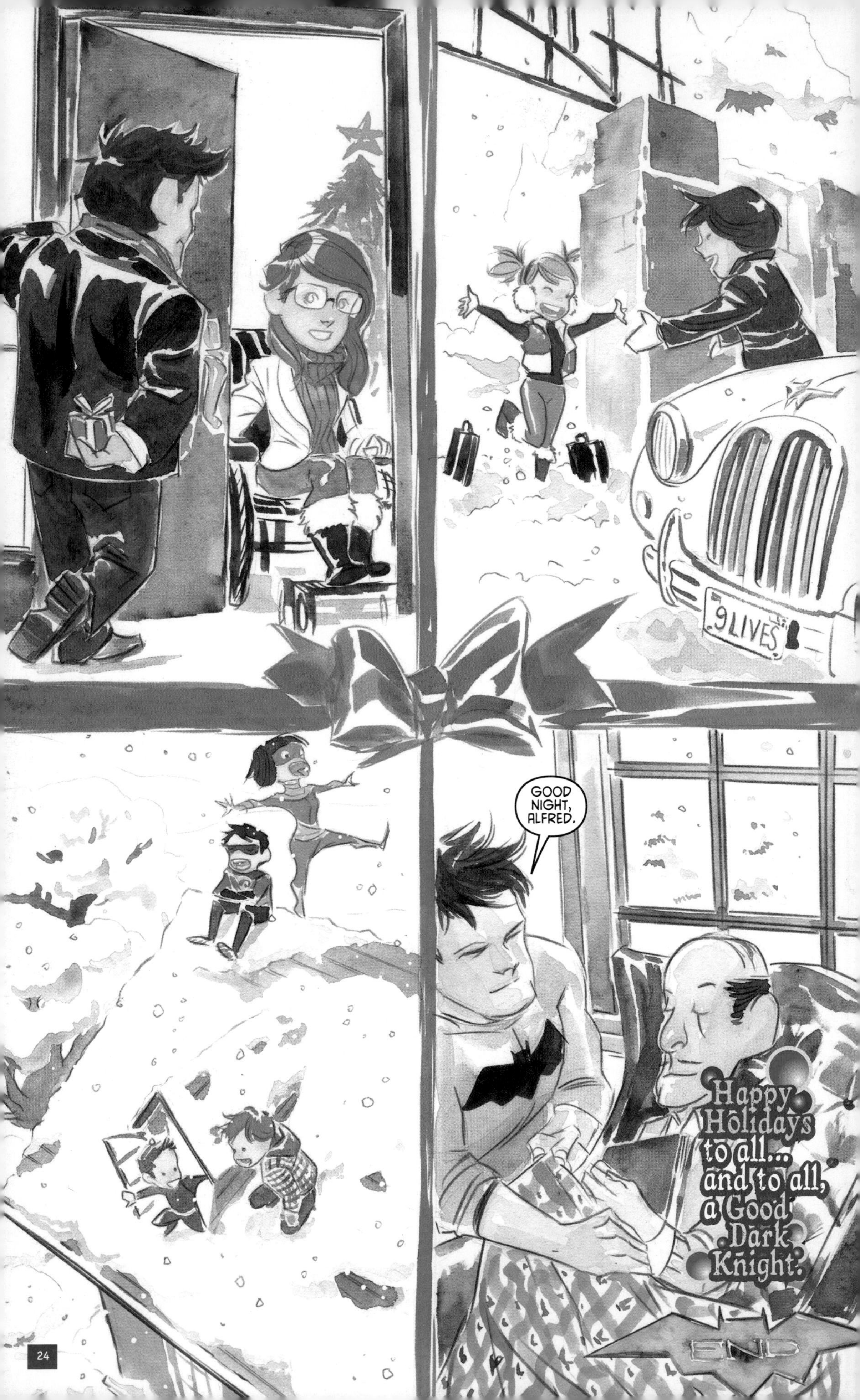
9 LIVES
GOOD NIGHT, ALFRED.
Happy Holidays to all... and to all, a Good Dark Knight.
END

CREATORS

DUSTIN NGUYEN — CO-WRITER & ILLUSTRATOR

Dustin Nguyen is an American comic artist whose body of work includes Wildcats v3.0, The Authority Revolution, Batman, Superman/ Batman, Detective Comics, Batgirl, and his creator owned project Manifest Eternity. Currently, he produces all the art for Batman: Li'l Gotham, which is also written by himself and Derek Fridolfs. Outside of comics, Dustin moonlights as a conceptual artist for toys, games, and animation. In his spare time, he enjoys sleeping, driving, and sketching things he loves.

DEREK FRIDOLFS — CO-WRITER

Derek Fridolfs is a comic book writer, inker, and artist. He resides in Gotham--present and future.

GLOSSARY

adequate (AD-i-kwit)--good enough for some need or requirement

aroma (uh-ROH-muh)--scent

doppelganger (DAW-puhl-gang-uhr)--someone who looks like someone else, or a ghastly duplicate of a living person

horseradish (HORHSS-rad-ish)--a strong and spicy sauce made from the root of the horseradish plant

infernal (in-FER-nuhl)--from the fiery depths, or very bad and unpleasant

midst (MIDSST)--if you are in the midst of something, you are in the middle part or area of it

molten (MOHL-ten)--melted by heat

mutating (MYOO-tay-ting)--to change and cause an unusual characteristic to develop in a plant or animal or human

relish (RELL-ish)--enjoy

sacrificial (sak-ruh-FISH-uhl)--of or relating to a sacrifice. A sacrifice is the act of giving up something that you want to keep especially in order to get or do something else or to help someone.

solace (SAHL-iss)--someone or something that gives a feeling of comfort to a person who is sad, depressed, etc.

VISUAL QUESTIONS & PROMPTS

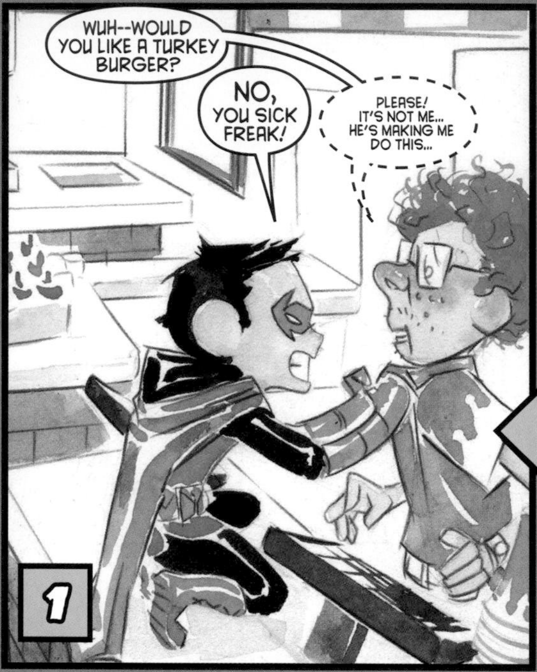
WUH--WOULD YOU LIKE A TURKEY BURGER?
NO, YOU SICK FREAK!
PLEASE! IT'S NOT ME... HE'S MAKING ME DO THIS...
1

1. Why does the red-haired kid's speech balloon have smaller text and a dotted outline?

2. This page has four panels. What is different about the panel borders in this page? Why do you think the artists did it this way?

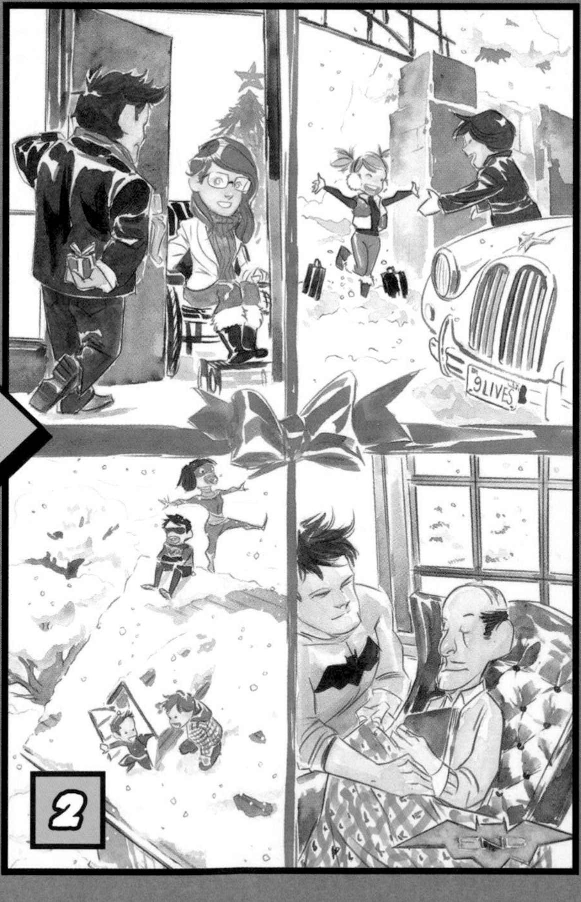
9LIVES
2

3. Based on the image in this panel, what do you think the word "doppelganger" means? Check your answer against the definition in the Glossary of this book.

"OR IN BATTLE AGAINST DUPLICATE DOPPELGÄNGERS FROM SOME DARK DIMENSION.

3

4. Out of all the family photos in Alfred's album, which is your favorite? Why?

4

BATMAN™
LI'L GOTHAM

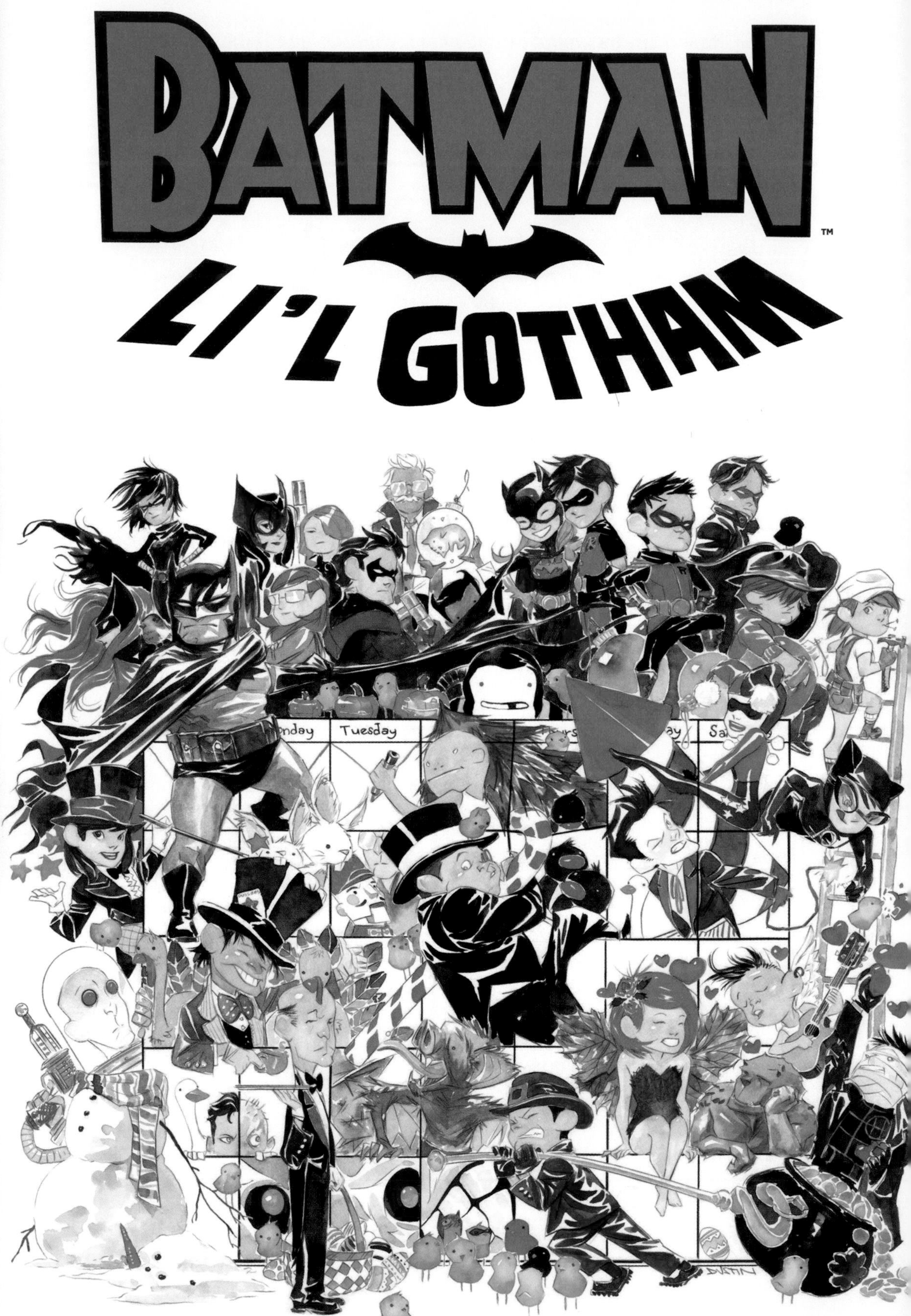
Tuesday

READ THEM ALL!

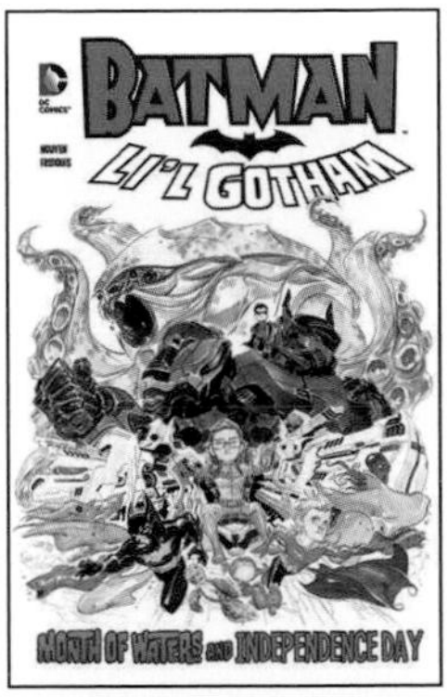
BATMAN
LI'L GOTHAM
MONTH OF WATERS AND INDEPENDENCE DAY

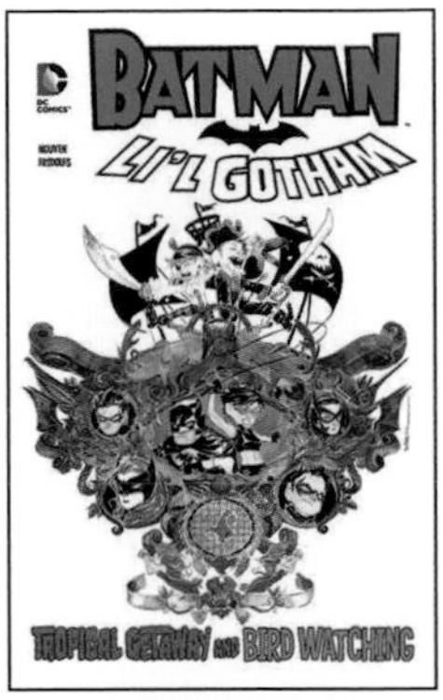
BATMAN
LI'L GOTHAM
TROPICAL GETAWAY AND BIRD WATCHING

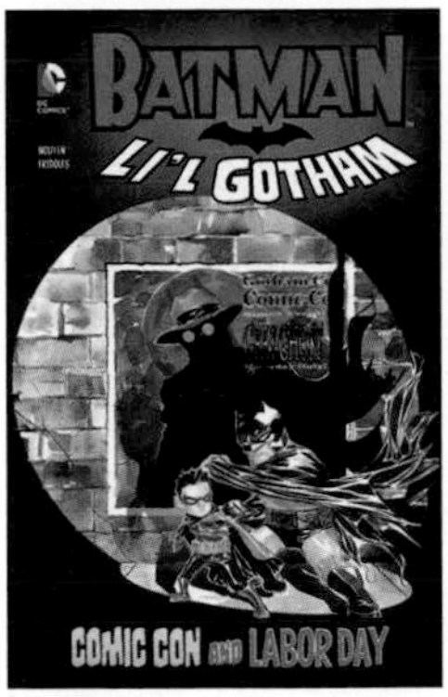
BATMAN
LI'L GOTHAM
COMIC CON AND LABOR DAY

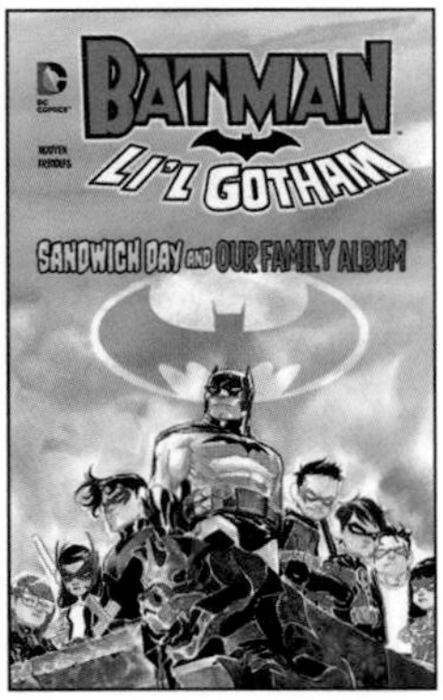
BATMAN
LI'L GOTHAM
SANDWICH DAY AND OUR FAMILY ALBUM

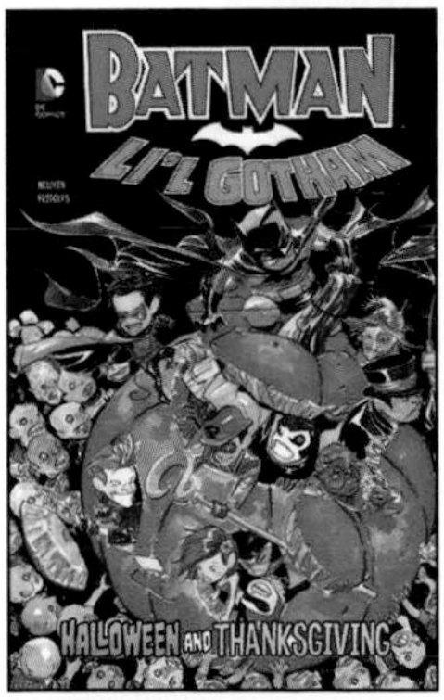
BATMAN
LI'L GOTHAM
HALLOWEEN AND THANKSGIVING

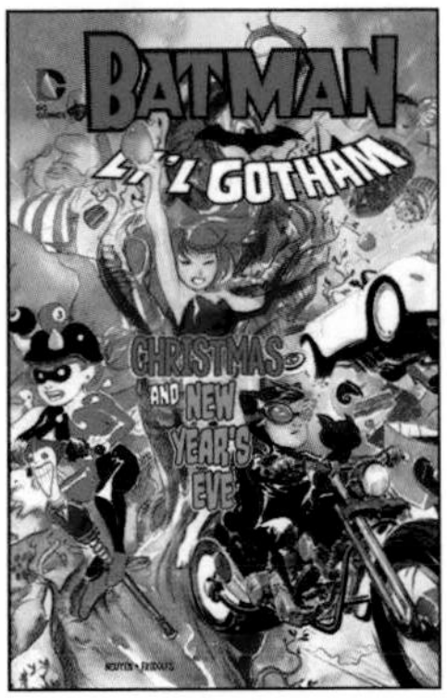
BATMAN
LI'L GOTHAM
CHRISTMAS AND NEW YEAR'S EVE

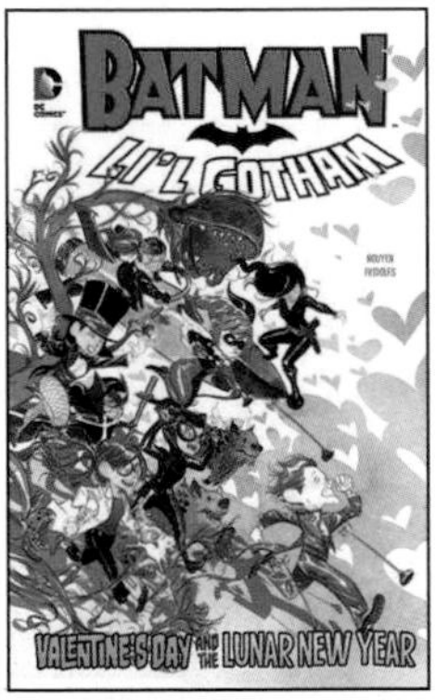
BATMAN
LI'L GOTHAM
VALENTINE'S DAY AND THE LUNAR NEW YEAR

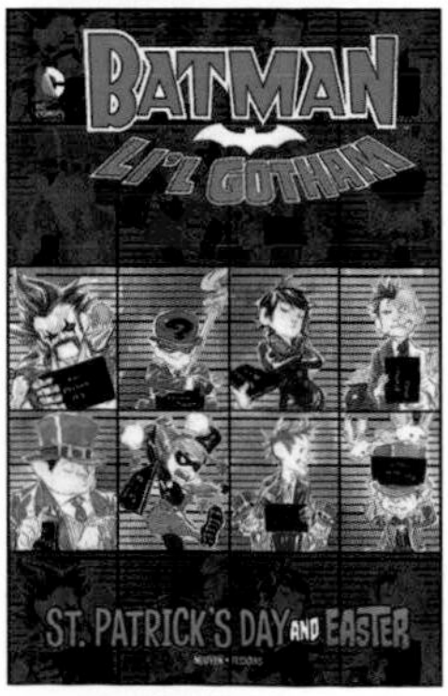
BATMAN
LI'L GOTHAM
ST. PATRICK'S DAY AND EASTER

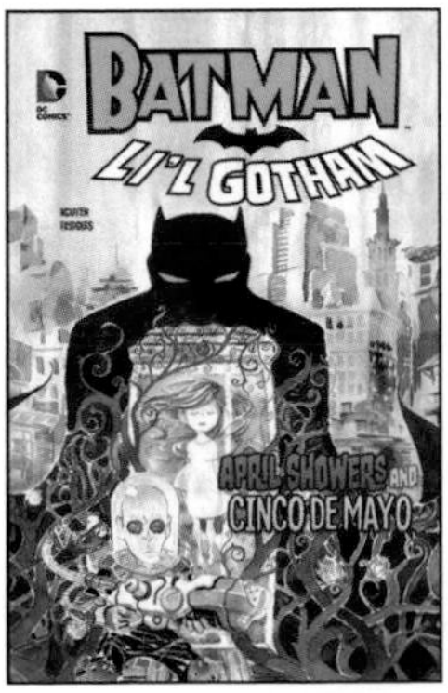
BATMAN
LI'L GOTHAM
APRIL SHOWERS AND CINCO DE MAYO

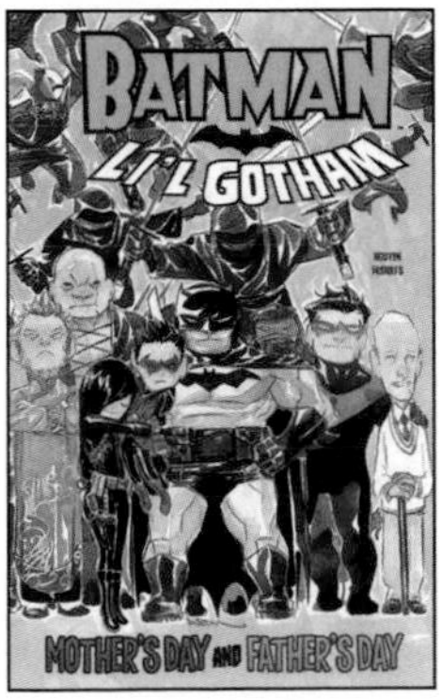
BATMAN
LI'L GOTHAM
MOTHER'S DAY AND FATHER'S DAY

BATMAN™
LI'L GOTHAM

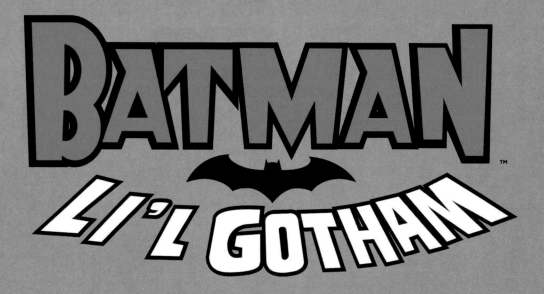